On The Rocks

Cozy Mystery filled with
Claws, Paws, and Clues: Where
Small-Town Secrets Unravel with a
Whisker of Whimsy!
Anna K Payne

AP Creations

Contents

Dedication

To my sweet husband, who always perks up at the thought of Morro Bay.

Chapter 1

The Boat Crash

Wilson arrived at the harbor with his officers just as the Coast Guard pulled their response boat from the dock. "Where are they going?" Wilson muttered.

Noah pointed toward the beach, "Look at the crowd by the beach."

"Wilson!" Wilson turned to see George, the Harbor Master, walking toward him. "The Coast Guard took my last man with him. I've got my radio on."

Wilson nodded to George, "Thanks, George. Noah, you and Julian, take my car to the beach. Make sure there isn't trouble over there."

Wilson walked with George back toward the harbor's office. "What's going on, George? Exactly what happened to that boat?"

George shook his head, "The details are still scarce. All I know is the Coast Guard got a phone call. Some surfer saw a boat go down."

"No mayday from the boat?" Wilson asked.

George shrugged. "Like I said, I don't know."

Wilson walked into the Harbor Station with George and looked at the lone woman sitting amidst the empty desks. She nodded, and he smiled. "How's it going?"

She shook her head, glanced at George, then looked down at her desk. Wilson knew then that she was a Morro Watch volunteer and incognito at work. Wilson followed George into his office and closed the door.

"Okay, George, what's really happening?" Wilson asked as he slid into a chair.

"We think it might be a shark attack. Some tourists were probably fishing in the wrong spot. It's like they angered the darn sharks." George sighed. "Reminds me of the whale attacks from twenty years ago."

"A shark attack? That's not good. I wonder if we can get some idea of why they are attacking boats." Wilson murmured.

George laughed, "Sure, Wilson, let's take your dog out on a boat and have a confab."

Wilson grinned at George, "Ha, that would be something, right?"

"You are dreaming now, man, if we understood what the sea lions, sea otters, sharks, and whales were thinking. Well, we could sell tickets or something." George scoffed.

Wilson stood as he laughed, "Thanks for the laugh, George. I'd better check on my officers. Let me know if you hear anything."

George waved him off, and Wilson left the building. Donner and Festus met him at the door. Wilson shook his head. "Think you can talk to a shark?"

Donner tilted his head. Festus looked at him, and his tail fluffed. Wilson chuckled, "Scary proposition, Festus? I know, I know. Let's head over to the beach."

The trio made their way to the crowd on the beach. Festus whined, and Donner barked. Then Festus jumped on Donner's back. Wilson smiled, "Too far for a kitty, Festus?"

As they approached the outskirts of the crowd, Noah broke away and met them in the sand. "What's going on?" Wilson asked.

"Coast Guard just pulled two people out of the water. There's a shark out there, but he isn't attacking." Noah said. "It's odd. I don't know why the shark is still there."

"Hmm, yes, what about the boat?" Wilson asked.

"It's capsized but still floating. I think they'll turn it over and tow it to the harbor." Noah explained.

"Okay. I'll head back to the harbor then." Wilson said, "Unless there is a problem with the crowd?"

Noah shook his head, "No. Julian is standing at the edge of the beach. He and the lifeguard are keeping everyone on shore. But I don't think anyone wants in the water with the shark still there."

Wilson nodded. "Thanks, Noah. Keep me posted."

Wilson turned back toward the harbor, and Donner followed with Festus still on his back. "I wonder if I need to talk to the Coast Guard or George?"

Wilson looked down at Donner, "Stick close. We'll finagle a boat somehow."

Chapter 2
The Shark Talk

"Why couldn't you have left me on shore, Donner? I can't type anything on the boat." Festus whined.

Donner shook his head as the fine spray of the waves hit his side. "Wilson brought a tablet with him. So, you will type."

Wilson approached and picked up Festus, "Let's get you set up in the cabin. It's warmer in there." Festus sighed as Wilson took him into the cabin and set him on a table with raised edges. A tablet rested there waiting for him. Then Festus heard Donner bark and knew he would be able to listen to him through the window.

Grumbling, Festus tapped on the tablet and opened a note. He filled in the basics, such as when and where he was taking down the note.

Wilson walked out of the cabin and hurried to Donner's side. The captain announced the shark on the starboard side. Donner moved to the railing and looked out over the water. He barked quietly. A shark swam close to the boat.

"Dude, you talking to me? I ain't never talked to a dog before." The shark said.

Donner huffed and answered, "Hey. Did you capsize that boat?"

"Naw, dog, the great white shark did. Those idiots in the boat pointed their harpoons straight at him. So he tipped them over. I swam around the boat until he left." The shark said.

"A great white whale, you say. I wonder why they were down here?" Donner asked.

The shark wheezed, "The water is warm for this season. The fish are plentiful. They must have thought they had arrived."

"They?" Donner asked.

"Sure. There was a whole pod. After the issue with the boat, they moved south again." The shark said.

"Thanks, shark. I appreciate the information. And thank you for looking out for the people in the water. You might want to take off now." Donner said.

The shark looked around, "Yeah, the people are out of the water, and the other boat towed the wreck away. I hope those idiots get fined."

Donner stared at the water where the shark had been. He looked around but didn't see the shark. Donner turned and hurried to the door to the cabin. Wilson opened the door, and both of them went in. "I told the captain to return to the harbor," Wilson said. "So, what did the shark say?"

Donner spoke with Felix as Felix tapped the screen. Wilson leaned over Felix and read as he typed. "A great white whale pod. Hmm, I'll make sure those people get fined." Wilson mumbled.

When Festus quit typing, Wilson emailed the note to himself. "Thanks, boys, good job."

Wilson, Donner, and Festus stood near the railing as the boat approached the dock. Wilson called thanks to the captain, who pulled away to resume his fishing. Wilson walked to the Coast Guard office and stepped inside.

"May I help you, Chief Wilson?" said the man at the front desk.

"Do you have those two from the boat accident here?" Wilson asked.

"I sure do, Wilson. Come on back here. I'm getting some complaints from those boys. They claim it was a whale that hit them." A Coast Guard official waved Wilson forward.

"I think you should believe them that it was a whale. I think the shark was protecting them. You'll probably verify that from the boat damage." Wilson said. "I've got a report of a pod of Great Whites swimming by. Those idiots turned their harpoons at them."

The Coast Guard officer's eyebrows lifted. "That is a criminal offense. I need to talk to this witness of yours."

Wilson shook his head, "Anonymous, but someone I trust. He doesn't want to be known as a snitch."

The man sighed, "Okay. I'll take your word for it. I'll get them fined and take away their boating permits for 90 days.

Wilson nodded, "Thank you. I appreciate it. I'm going to check on my men."

"Thanks for your help, Wilson. Wish I had your resources." The Officer said.

Wilson left the Coast Guard facility and patted Donner on the head. "Good job, boys. Mission accomplished."

Chapter 3
Halloween Approaches

After a few months, Julian attempts to flirt with Sharon's neighbor, Mary.

Julian leaned toward Mary, and she blushed. "Julian," Mary looked for her boss, "You are breathing on the cookies. Step back."

"So," Julian began again, "Halloween is coming up. Were you here for last Halloween?"

Mary shook her head, "No, I came in November. That's when the house became available."

"Oh, okay. Well, they do this paddleboard thing on Halloween. People dress up as witches and paddle around the bay for a few hours. We had over a hundred last year, even with the pandemic." Julian said.

"That makes sense. Paddling on the bay is outside, and keeping six feet apart is easy." Mary said.

"Do you paddleboard?" Julian asked.

Mary shook her head, "I work on Halloween. Online all day and then the evening shift here."

Julian nodded, "Right, I'm on duty starting at noon. That's when people start showing up."

Mary smiled, "I do have a costume, though."

"Really? If your costume is a princess, that won't work; that's what you are every day." Julian wiggled his eyebrows.

Mary laughed, "I'll be a candy cane."

"Oooh, delicious sounding. I'll be sure to patrol by for a taste." Julian waved as he walked out the door.

Her boss walked in from the kitchen, "Hmm. Did you pack all those cookies while he was flirting with you? I'm not sure I could've moved." She waved her hand in front of her face. "He's definitely hot. Has he asked you on a date yet?"

Mary's face felt hot, "No. He hasn't. You think he will?"

Her boss nodded, "Sure do. I bet he was making sure no one asked you out tomorrow while he's working."

Mary sighed, "He is awfully cute."

Her boss slanted her a look, "So are you, honey, so are you. There's the timer!"

Her boss disappeared back into the kitchen while Mary finished packing the box of cookies. She carefully labeled it and set it on a shelf for later.

Then a crowd of people entered, and Mary said, "Hi, welcome to the Cookie Crumbles. Let me know if I can be of any help."

***

Olivia shoved Julian over and stood at the front desk before her computer. "What are you doing back in already? Did you ask Mary out yet?"

Julian ducked his head, "Uh, no, she's working Halloween. So, I guess I'll have to wait until November."

Olivia frowned at her computer, "You should ask her out a few days ahead so she can prepare."

"I should?" Julian asked.

"Definitely," Wilson said from behind him. "Women like to plan."

"That's not what Nancy says." Julian put his hands on his hips.

"Watch it, young whippersnapper. I'll put you on nights indefinitely." Wilson said with a grin.

"Ha ha, I'm on nights all this week," Julian said.

"Yes, you are. Sharon is doing the schedule again. It's very evenly distributed." Wilson sighed. "Finally."

"Have you heard anything about a new chief, Chief?" Olivia asked.

"Why do you keep frowning at the screen, Olivia? And no, nothing yet. If this keeps up, I will forget what I was doing for retirement." Wilson said.

Wilson and Julian both leaned over Olivia to see the screen. "Guys, why don't you just ask me to move?" Olivia huffed.

"Because you need to keep answering those texts. Julian, do you see the one out at the state park? Go check that out." Wilson ordered.

Julian sighed, "Yes, sir, Chief. I'm outta here."

"I certainly hope this doesn't mean a busy Halloween night. I'm dressing up as a warrior. Nancy's idea. I'm going to regret it." Wilson muttered as he walked away. "Let me know if something else happens that Julian can't cover."

Chapter 4

Halloween Morning

Donner sighed as Wilson added the final touches to Donner's costume. Then Wilson frowned into the mirror. "I look ridiculous. But Nancy said."

Donner huffed quietly, and Wilson glared at him. "No laughing from the gallery." Wilson moved to the door and laughed, "Look at Festus and Pete! At least you look respectable, Donner. Festus is Snoopy in a pumpkin costume. Pete is Charlie Brown. I need a picture of this one."

Wilson locked up his house, and he and Donner moved down the sidewalk. Festus skittered sideways behind Pete, his human. "Donner, you look scary! What happened to you?" Festus stuttered.

Donner slowly smiled, making Festus squeak. "Yikes, that's even scarier. Don't do that!"

Donner huffed quietly. "I'm a wolf, Festus. It's just a costume."

"Yeah, well, my human is some kid named Charlie, and I'm supposed to be his dog in costume. I hate the floppy ears. Some kid already ran up to me and hugged me. My fur is sticky. Yuck." Festus complained.

Donner stepped behind Wilson and Pete, "Come on, Festus, I mean, Snoopy. Keep up."

Festus grumbled as he loped into place. "I don't know where Pete gets these ideas. I figured he'd be the Marshal, and I'd be his deputy."

Donner laughed, "That was last summer, re-member? You scared those criminals into running."

Festus mumbled, "I remember. I got a mes-sage from Myra. She said things have been busy. And they are going to get busier for her. The vet is bringing over kittens and an injured mother for her to take care of."

"She's a nurse now?" Donner shook his head, "They stay busy. They've always got stuff happening. No one's been shot, though?"

"Naw, the mother and kittens were saved from a fire up north of here. Pretty scary business. I hope we don't get a fire near here." Festus sighed.

"Not likely here, but it depends on whether we get more rain. Suppose there's a lightning strike, wind, or some silly tourist. We do have woods and shrubs that would burn." Donner squinted at the sky. "It looks like we'll have sunshine today. That's good for the tourists."

Wilson's radio put out a burst of static. Wilson talked into it, "What's up, Olivia?"

"Julian came in early, so I will take off for a few hours. I need sustenance." Olivia's voice came through the radio.

"That was nice of Julian. Wonder what he's up to?" Wilson muttered. Then he spoke into the radio, "That's for the update, Olivia."

Wilson glanced at Pete, "Mind if I ask you a personal question?"

Pete eyed Wilson for a second and said, "How personal?" He grimaced.

Wilson laughed, "Where do you get all of those costumes for Festus? The pumpkin one was pretty scary for some people, but this has him looking like Snoopy."

Pete grinned, "And I'm Charlie Brown," he puffed out his chest. "I can't wait to see Lucy."

Wilson raised his eyebrows, "There's a Lucy?"

Pete laughed, "There's always a Lucy." He looked around for listening ears, "I got the first few online from, you know, Amazon, but I got to know one of the companies selling the costumes. Now, I order directly from her.

She makes me original costumes no one else has."

"Wow," Wilson said and shook his head. "I see. Are you still watching Gunsmoke re-runs?"

"As if! I finally bought the DVDs so I can watch without all those commercials." Pete said. "It was pricey but worth it. I hate watch-ing the boring ones."

"Right, the boring ones. And the other not-so-boring ones?" Wilson asked.

"That's why there's YouTube, silly, keep up, man!" Pete exclaimed.

"Well, thanks for the information," Wilson said.

Pete looked back at Donner, "Where did you get the dog's costume?"

Wilson shrugged, "Nancy got it. She thought it was cute."

Pete frowned, "It's not cute, it's downright terrifying. Keep him away from little kids."

They arrived at the coffee shop, and Wilson paused, "Want me to buy you a coffee?"

Pete shook his head, "Naw, I'm heading to the boardwalk to look for Lucy."

"You mean there is an actual Lucy?" Wilson asked.

"I'll never tell." Pete waved and made a turn toward the harbor.

Felix turned to follow him, but Donner barked. "What are you two doing?"

Felix rolled his eyes, "Pete found a girlfriend. She said she'd meet him on the boardwalk."

Felix turned and loped after Pete. He yowled over his shoulder. "I'm part of his costume."

Donner huffed and pushed Wilson toward the cafe door. "I'm going. Pete and some Lucy, huh? A mystery to solve, right, Donner?"

Wilson opened the door, and Donner stepped into the cafe and sighed, "There she is," he whined softly. Wilson stood next to Donner and stared at Nancy. She smiled and waved at him.

"I've got your coffee right here and a tidbit for Donner," Nancy called. She turned back to the customer at the counter. "Did you decide?"

The customer shook her head. Something about her seemed familiar, but he couldn't quite place it. The woman turned her head to look at Wilson and said, "You can serve the Chief first."

When she looked at Wilson again, he saw the mask around her neck. Then he under-stood. She wore a royal blue old-fashioned dress, patent leather shoes, and cuffed socks. Her hair was dark, almost black, with an odd shape to it. "It's Lucy," Wilson breathed.

Donner nudged Wilson impatiently. "Fine, fine, not supposed to stare anyway." Wilson walked up to the counter and nodded at Lucy. Then he turned to Nancy and handed over a ten-dollar bill. "Thanks for the tidbit. Donner is waiting." He gathered his coffee and the tiny sack for Donner. "I'll see you later."

Nancy grinned. "The costume looks great, Wilson, and Donner looks very realistic."

Lucy turned to look at Donner, "Oh, that's a costume? I thought he was a wolf." She asked Wilson, "Do you think I could check it out? I make costumes."

Wilson grinned, and things fell into place, "Sure, Donner won't mind. He's actually a German Shepherd police dog."

They walked up to Donner, and she carefully touched Donner's costume. "I see. Very clever. Very clever. That's a great idea. I didn't think about doing it that way." She looked up at Wilson. "Thanks for letting me look." Then she returned to the counter, "I'll take the peppermint hot chocolate, heavy on the peppermint, please. And a croissant."

Nancy rang up the total and quickly made the hot chocolate. Wilson and Donner walked out the door. Wilson pulled out an apple slice and handed it to Donner. Donner wolfed it down. Then Wilson continued his slow walk down to the harbor.

Chapter 5
The Witch Brigade

Donner searched the boardwalk for Festus and his human. He and Wilson turned onto the boardwalk to walk, but Wilson was immediately pulled aside.

"Wilson, how's it going? Expecting trouble today?" The oversized man laughed loudly and slapped Wilson on his back.

"No, I'm hoping for a calm day. Something like the waters in the bay." Wilson gestured toward the water.

The man looked Wilson up and down, coming to rest on Donner. "I get the dog being a wolf, but are you some kind of Indian?"

"Very good, John, you guessed it. I'm a warrior from ancient times." Wilson said absently.

"Nancy picked it out, right? She sure is something. You moved in on her pretty quickly. Beat the rest of us to her side." John shook his head.

"Now, John, what would your Margaret say about that?" Wilson's eyes twinkled.

"My Margaret is one of a kind. I never would have strayed. You know I was joking. You won't tell her, will you?" John's eyes widened in panic.

"Relax, John. I'll never tell." Wilson laughed and walked a few feet. "See you later, John. Say hi to Margaret for me."

Donner walked behind Wilson as a group of tourists hurried past them. He still hadn't seen Felix yet. When they came to a bench, Wilson sat down and sipped his coffee. "Look at all those paddleboarders. I bet the shopkeepers are happy with that. Good for business."

Donner sat next to Wilson beside the bench and stared at the large number of paddle-boards and humans congregating in the bay. Humans think of the weirdest things to do. Dress up in costumes and get on a paddle-board. Donner huffed.

"Now, what are those sea lions yelling about?" Wilson mused. Donner turned his attention to the sea lion barge. The barge gave the sea lions a place to congregate other than on the boardwalk and on boats. They filled it to full capacity, and it seemed they had never stopped moving.

"There's the sheriff over there with his dog." Said one sea lion. "Hey, Donner, what's hang-ing? Why do you look meaner today?" Several sea lions laughed loudly.

"It's the dress-up day, Lionel. Didn't you know that? Hollow Wieners Day. People dress up and say trick or treat, and then they give them food." Hugh said.

Lionel looked at Hugh, "Oh, so that's what all the noise is about. Well, dumb humans are interrupting my nap."

Hugh reared up and pushed Lionel over, making him fall into the water. "That shut you up."

Donner huffed again. The silly sea lions. He shook his head. A voice spoke beside him, "Hey, Donner. The sea lions are having a talkative day."

Donner whipped his head around and laughed. "What happened to you, Festus?"

"What? What are you talking about, Donner? Lucy brought me some bacon from the coffee shop. I hate to fight off a couple of seagulls. They didn't get any." Festus said. When he sat down, the bird poo dribbled off his costume onto his back. Festus groaned.

Donner shook with laughter and tried to look serious. "It appears they gave you more than they got."

Wilson looked down and said, "Yuck, Festus. Here, I got a tissue in my pocket." He pulled out a soft white piece of paper and wiped off Festus's costume and back. "Those seagulls sure do give you a hard time. I guess Pete found his Lucy."

Festus sighed, "Yep. Pete is with Lucy, and now I'm stuck in this costume. At least it isn't too warm, and it's not raining."

"Where did Pete and Lucy go?" Donner asked.

"I think they went home. I didn't go with them because they acted all lovey-dovey." Festus said.

"Good, you can help me patrol the board-walk. Wilson should get up and make another lap." Donner said. He let out a quiet bark and stared at Wilson.

Wilson drained his coffee cup and put it in the receptacle. "Time for our sentry duty. Keep an eye out for trouble, boys."

When they walked around the corner, it became apparent how many visitors and townspeople had turned out for the contest. The bay was so crowded that most boarders were busy trying to maneuver around the other paddleboards.

Festus trotted next to Donner, "Wow, I think that is the best turnout we've ever had. I'm not sure I can count that high. Oh, look, there's a blue witch."

Donner checked to see where Festus pointed and shook his head, "I hope they don't get makeup in the bay. There will be so many complaints. Even their hands and neck are blue."

"Oh, I see a green one and a purple one too. The yellow one doesn't have makeup, but she still looks good. What's wrong with that cat?" Festus asked.

"That's not a real cat, Festus. Calm down. No one would take their cat on a paddleboard." Donner huffed.

"I think I see a couple of dogs with costumes on. I hope they don't fall off." Festus said.

"Me too. The water's too cold for a rescue. Besides, I'll ruin my costume." Donner chuckled.

"I think they are making an announcement. Yep, I'm gonna put my paws over my ears." Festus said just as the loudspeaker blared.

"Settle down, folks. Quiet on shore. Let's have the paddleboards line up to parade by the judges' booth. Everyone paddle down to those trees over there. Harry hung a starting sign on the tree. Let's do the witches first again. That worked out great last year." The mayor paused and spoke with the man next to him. "Right, make sure your number is clearly visible to shore. That will be on your right side."

The mayor stepped down and walked to the judges' booth. The three people sitting there nodded to the mayor and then shuffled the papers in front of them.

A single-file line of paddleboards trekked up the bay toward the judges' table. The judges watched them, marked their papers, and added notes.

Wilson moved to a railing and leaned against it. Donner and Festus lie down. Festus ended on his face, and Donner used his forepaw to push his rear end down. "Thanks, Donner," Festus said. Wilson's eyes roved over the crowd on the boardwalk, looking for anything unusual. Donner kept an eye on the seagulls and sea lions, just in case they butted into the ceremony.

Festus's eyes slowly closed, and he quietly snored. Donner placed his back paw on Festus's tail, trying to keep him steady. When he turned back to the bay, he let out a sharp bark. Wilson looked at Donner, whose nose was pointed toward the bay. "What's he think he's doing?" Wilson exclaimed.

Wilson took out his phone and pulled up the Harbor Master. "George, what is that boat doing?"

"Trying to get away from the Coast Guard. Get those people out of the way." George yelled. "Mayor, get those paddleboards on shore now!"

Wilson raced down toward the beach area and called Olivia, "Olivia. Emergency down here. Get rescue squads, medics, and all available officers down here now!"

Chapter 6

The Aftermath

It all happened at once. Festus watched Donner as he raced toward the water's edge and deflected a paddleboard. Then Donner nuzzled the toddler he'd protected while he searched for his mother.

When the baby's hands clenched into his fur, he experimentally took a few steps, leading the tiny human away from the water. A man rushed up and grabbed the baby, turning to search for his wife. "Good doggie." He muttered, but Donner had already raced away.

Wilson plowed into the waves, dodging paddleboards and pulling people ashore. "Move back, make room," he shouted.

Julian raced into the waves further away, swimming out to a struggling paddleboarder.

Festus saw Noah, dressed in a burlap sack, run down the beach and into the waves. Another big wave knocked more of the paddleboarders into the water.

Festus searched the bay for the boats and saw the first swing wide in a circle, causing another bigger wake. Festus saw Julian disappear under the water and reappear after the wave. Julian dragged a woman behind him, her paddleboard still attached to her ankle. But Festus couldn't find Donner, Wilson, or Noah.

Just then, the boat revved its engine, drowning out the people's screams, and sliced through the bay, heading straight for the Coast Guard boat blocking the exit.

The water moved the Coast Guard boat at the last minute, and the other ship slipped by. A huge wave hit the bay entrance as the boat made its escape. The force of the wave broke up the ship, and the men on the boat were tossed into the water.

A great white whale surfaced in an impressive leap, landing on the men in the water. Then, the whale dived back into the water, disappearing from view.

The Coast Guard began fishing the men out of the water. Festus looked back at the beach and found Donner beside Wilson on the ground next to a man. Festus hopped on top of a random statue to see better. It was Noah on the ground. A woman sat nearby, sobbing in a man's arms. Julian swam back out into the water to retrieve another paddleboarder. Sharon, in uniform, cleared the parking lot with the help of Jane, the new officer dressed as a witch. Her police dog, disguised as a princess, Susie, herded children nearby, keeping them out of the way while their parents were busy.

Donner trotted to Festus, "Hey, help Susie with the kids. They need a distraction." Then he ran off again.

Festus swallowed loudly. "Sure, Donner, I'll go let all the children maul my body." He shuddered and dropped to the ground.

As he approached Susie, she huffed, "Thanks, Festus. Go stand in the middle of my group, where those two girls are crying."

Festus looked at the mass of children and slipped through the knot of legs and arms. "Hey, there. I'm a cat dressed like a cartoon dog dressed like a pumpkin. Want to pet me?" Festus said bravely.

One girl wrapped her arms around his neck and sobbed into his Snoopy ears. Another little boy squeezed the pumpkin and giggled. "It's soft," he shouted. Several other children crowded around Festus, squeezing and touching him over and over.

Susie raced around the mass of children surrounding Festus, catching the stragglers from wandering away. Occasionally, adults would approach the group, calling out a name. Susie would trot toward them. If a child recognizes an adult, she lets them go. Susie would bark three times if the children weren't sure, getting Jane's attention.

Jane would run over to the adults and ask for their IDs. Usually, she let the child go with the adult reasonably quickly, but one little girl was adamantly opposed to leaving. She clung to Festus and refused the move. Jane sent Susie to get Wilson, who had migrated to the top of the beach near the street. Susie returned with Wilson in tow. Wilson nodded to the man, who was waiting impatiently. "Hi. Are you okay?"

The man jerked his head in a nod. Then looked at the little girl. Wilson crouched down next to Festus. "Hey, Festus, you did your part today. Good job." Then he looked at the little girl with her arms wrapped around Festus's neck. "Hey, sweetie. What's going on? Are you worried about something?"

The little girl pointed at the man and stated, "That's not my daddy. I don't know him."

"I see." Wilson looked at the man. "Sir, who are you?"

The man stepped forward, and the little girl slipped around Festus so she was standing next to Wilson. "No, I won't go," she said.

"I understand her hesitation perfectly. She hasn't met me before. I met her dad on the beach. I was watching my wife on her paddle-board, and he was watching his wife. We fell into conversation."

The man's voice broke, "My wife came out of the water with a hurt ankle and a bloody gash, but she was conscious and told me to meet her at the clinic."

He glanced at the little girl, "But her mommy didn't wake up when they pulled her ashore. And her dad looked at me and said, "Can you watch my baby?"

Wilson stood and placed his hand on the little girl's head. "Do you have a plan?"

"No, after her parents left in the ambulance, she ran away. I searched everywhere and finally saw her with this, uh, animal." The man scratched his head and stared at Festus.

Wilson chuckled, "This is Festus. Believe it or not, he's a cat. His owner buys him all kinds of costumes. Today, he is dressed like Snoopy, and Pete is like Charlie Brown."

"You're a cat," cried the little girl. "No wonder I love you."

Donner trotted up to Wilson and stopped next to Festus. The little girl whispered, "Big."

"This is my dog, Donner. He is friends with Festus. He likes little girls." Wilson said. "Look, I tell you what, why don't you leave the little girl with me while you round up your wife. This bandit here is actually my medical man, Mark. Mark, can you take this man to his wife at the clinic?"

Mark put out his hand to the man, "Hi. I'm Mark. Who are you, and is your car here at the beach?"

The man sighed, "I'm Ted. A man I was standing next to went in the ambulance to the hospital with his wife. He asked me to watch his little girl. But she doesn't know me."

Mark nodded, "Man, that's rough. Do you remember their names?"

Ted looked thoughtful. He glanced at the little girl. "Mark or Max and Iris or Irene?"

The little girl shook her head, almost knocking Festus down. "No, daddy is Bart, and Mommy is Eilene."

"Bart and Eilene, Bart and Eilene, hmmm." Mark leaned down toward the little girl. "What's your last name?"

"Hampton." The little girl said.

Mark nodded. "You just moved here, didn't you?" Mark looked at Wilson. "They moved into the condo near me. I've spoken with them a few times."

Ted relaxed and sighed. "That's good. I didn't even know that. My wife and I are staying at a hotel up the way. She sent me an email with the information." He pulled out his phone. "My wife won't be able to walk back to the hotel."

Mark clapped Ted on the back, "No worries, man, my car is here. I'll drive you to the clinic and drop you two off at your hotel. Let's head out now."

Ted looked uncertain, "But what about her..."

"She's going to stay with me, Festus, and Donner. In a little bit, Nancy will be back with her car. She can drive us to the hospital to find her parents." Wilson said.

Ted smiled for the first time. "Thanks, and tell Bart I tried."

Festus watched the man leave with Mark. He heaved a shaky breath. "Can someone get this little girl off of me? She's strangling me."

Donner huffed a laugh.

Chapter 7

The Little Girl

Wilson called what members of his team he could find into a meeting. "Sharon, why don't you check with the Harbor Master and the Coast Guard to discover what happened to our serene Halloween event?"

Sharon nodded, "Will do. Stay safe, everyone." Sharon walked away from the circle around Wilson.

"I can cover Noah's shift. Olivia is at the clinic with Noah." Julian said.

"Thank you, Julian. That's helpful. Who's on the front desk/watch duty?" Wilson asked.

Jane raised her hand. "That would be me. I should head back to the office now. Susie, let's go." Susie huffed a quiet goodbye to Donner and Festus as she trotted after Jane.

Wilson grinned at Julian. "It's great having so many officers available. It cuts down on my stress level."

Julian laughed, "I'll make a pass through the boardwalk. Make sure everything will be quiet tonight." Julian turned to scan the beach and nodded. "Looks like everyone is gone. Except for the Mayor. I'm off." He walked quickly away as the mayor arrived.

Wilson nodded at the mayor, "Mayor, is everyone accounted for?"

The mayor scratched his head, "I'm not sure." He dropped a pile of loose papers, and Donner promptly sat on them. "Oops. I had a list of the people in the contest, but I'm unsure how to tell if everyone is out of the water." He bent to gather his papers, and Donner stepped aside.

Wilson glanced at Donner. "Huh, that could be a problem. Only the seagulls know for sure. Did everyone have an emergency contact?"

The mayor wrinkled his forehead, "Now that's an idea. This is the list of contestants. Yes, my assistant has a column for emergency contact. I suppose I could start at the top of the list and call each one." He sighed, "Back to the office."

Wilson watched the mayor walk away slowly. He pulled out his phone and sent a text to Nancy, "Bring a tablet and be prepared to drive to the hospital in San Louie, please."

His phone dings as a seagull flies to the ground beside Donner. He checks and clicks a button, "Hey, Olivia, how's Noah?"

"The doctors refuse to release him unless he has someone to watch over him. And Noah says he's not going to the hospital. They are getting ready to close the clinic." Oliva complained.

Wilson grimaced, "Do you think you could stomach watching over Noah tonight?"

"Me? Uh, I don't know him that well, but I can argue him under the table. Sure, I'll do that. Good idea, Chief." Olivia said.

Wilson heard Olivia talking to someone. Then, muffled shouting. "Chief? Olivia is not staying with me. I'm fine. I wasn't out that long." Noah said.

Wilson pulled out his Chief tone of voice, "That's not what the doctors are saying there, now is it? Olivia is the person we have available to babysit you. You will allow her to monitor you during the night. Is that clear?"

"Sir, yes, sir. Here's Olivia." Noah said.

Then Olivia came back on the line, "Thanks, Chief. I've got the lowdown from the doctor, nurse, and all the paperwork. They gave us some samples for tonight. Okay, I'll be at Noah's place."

Olivia ended the call, and Wilson chuckled. "What's so funny, mister?" The little girl asked.

"Well, now, I'm thinking Noah has a crush on Olivia. It will be interesting to see how that works out. And you did very well waiting for me to finish everything. Is Festus still breathing?" Wilson asked.

The little girl giggled, "Of course he is. I can feel his breath on my neck. Are we going to go find my daddy now?"

"Yes, as soon as Nancy arrives. She's going to drive us in her car." Wilson said.

"Can Festus come too?" She asked as Festus squeaked.

"Yes. Let me call Pete and check." Wilson pulled out his phone again and punched another button. "Yo, Pete, how's it going? We had a bit of a dust-up here, and I have to take a run to the hospital. Is it okay if I take Festus along? Are you sure? Okay, thanks. Yes, I'll deliver him to your door later."

Wilson looked at his phone and shook his head. "I heard a woman in the background. I bet it was Lucy. And he said Festus can go with us." Wilson smiled at the little girl. "Is it okay if I ask for your name?"

The little girl looked steadily at Wilson and nodded. "My name is Sarah. It has an h at the end."

"That's a good, solid name, Sarah. It fits you." Wilson said.

Chapter 8

The Car Ride

A car pulled into the parking lot and stopped next to Wilson. Donner trotted to the car and grinned. "Hello, My Precious. You are looking very golden."

The golden cat in the car preened and pawed at the gold band around her neck. "I'm supposed to be a gold ring."

Wilson opened the back door and helped Sarah into the back seat. He had to pick up Festus and place the cat next to the girl, who still refused to let go of Festus. Nancy turned around and smiled at the little girl.

"You have really weird ears! Are those real?" Sarah asked.

Nancy laughed and shook her head, "No, I'm wearing a costume. I'm a Hobbit. It's a character from a book. And my cat is my gold ring. Her name is My Precious."

Sarah looked at My Precious, and her eyes grew wide. "Is she made of gold? Or fur?"

"She's a real cat. You can touch her fur if you ask nicely." Nancy said.

Sarah said softly, "May I touch your fur?"

My Precious butted her head gently on Sarah's arm. Then she batted her eyes at Festus. "Hello, handsome," and Festus whined.

Sarah laughed, "I don't think the gold kitty will hurt you, Festus. She seems nice."

Wilson got into the passenger seat and looked at Nancy. "Did you bring the tablet?"

Nancy nodded, "It's in the very back. Festus can type while I drive. If you can replace him with Donner." Nancy pulled out onto the road and turned toward the freeway.

Wilson leaned around the seat and looked at the animals. "Festus needs to fill out a report for me in the back. Would Donner or My Precious be a good replacement?" He asked Sarah.

Sarah looked at the large German Shepherd on the floor next to her. "Donner is very big. If he puts his head on my lap, I can hold him. I'm not sure the gold kitty wants me to hold her." She whispered loudly.

Sarah let go of Festus, who jumped into the hatchback's back compartment. "Does Festus really know how to type?"

"Yes, he does. But we don't tell anyone. People wouldn't understand. But I think you are safe and can keep a secret." Wilson said.

"Oh, no. You did not just say that, Wilson!" Nancy exclaimed. She looked into the rear view mirror at Sarah, "You can tell your parents about Festus. We don't want to keep secrets from them." She glared at Wilson. "Nothing scares a parent faster than a kid keeping a secret with another adult."

Wilson opened his mouth and shut it. "I'm sorry, I didn't mean to do that. I just don't want people to blab it about. Someone might try to steal Festus or do experiments on him. That's all."

Sarah nodded, "I understand. It's not a bad secret. It's keeping Festus safe."

Nancy shook her head, "Just how old are you, Sarah? You seem very mature."

"Thank you. I am almost four." Sarah said.

"Four? Is that all? You sound more like you are six or seven." Nancy said.

Sarah sighed, "My mom says I'm preco, pre-cocious, and I must be polite. I'm sorry if I wasn't."

"No, you've been very polite," Wilson said. "So you haven't been to school yet?"

Sarah shook her head, "I used to go to preschool, but we couldn't afford it after we moved here. I hang out with my mom or dad, and sometimes at their jobs. Sometimes it's boring, but I've read three books since we moved."

"You read?" Nancy asked. "What kind of books do you like?"

"I like the Narnia books. I've read those twice. I'm getting a new book for my birthday. It's by an author who was friends with CS Lewis. I can't remember his name." Sarah said.

Nancy stuttered, "You, you, CS Lewis, I bet you are talking about Tolkien. He wrote about Hobbits. He's my favorite author."

"Yes, that's the name. Maybe we can talk about the books after I start reading them. Mommy and Daddy don't have time to read like I do. They haven't even read The Silver Chair." Sarah said.

"I love Puddleglum. He is so pessimistic, he's funny." Nancy laughed.

"Yes, and he looks like a frog." Sarah giggled.

Wilson looked from Nancy to Sarah, "It appears I need to read the Chronicles of Narnia. I've only read the first one."

"The first one is good, but it isn't my favorite. Puddleglum is my favorite character after Aslan, of course." Sarah said.

"Of course," agreed Nancy.

"But I liked the trip on the boat too. And the end of the world. Oh, and the beginning of the world. And A Horse and His Boy!" Sarah bounced a little, and Donner gagged. "Oh, sorry, Donner. I get excited when I can talk about my stories."

Donner huffed, and Festus squeaked. "Is Festus okay? Oh, Festus, that's a nice cover for your tablet."

Festus managed to avoid both the little girl and My Precious on his way to Wilson. Once Wilson took the tablet, he climbed onto Wilson's lap. "Oh, okay, thank you, Festus."

Wilson began reading and pulled out his phone. "Julian? Where are you?" Julian started talking, and Wilson cut him off, "Never mind, get back to the beach. Get Sharon to meet you there. We have another body in the bay. No, I don't think so. I'm not sure. Look, just watch the water when you get close to the edge, and the seagulls will gather around the body."

Wilson sighed, "I'm not sure. But a couple of sea otters are guarding the body. Make sure they move away before you try to grab it. Right, yes, you'll need a boat. Thanks, Julian. Keep me posted."

Nancy looked at Wilson, "You missed somebody?"

"It sure looks like it. Everything was chaos, but I thought we had everyone. I'll have to check with the Mayor once Julian and Sharon retrieve the body." Wilson said.

"Somebody died?" Sarah asked.

"It looks like it. We aren't sure." Wilson said.

"And Donner talked to the seagulls and told Festus, who told you. That's cool. I could write my own stories about you guys." Sarah shook her head, "But no one would believe it. I'd have to sell it as fiction."

Nancy pulled into a busy parking lot and found a place to park. "Okay, we are at the hospital. How are we going to do this?" Nancy asked.

"Mr Wilson will take me in and find my daddy." Sarah sat up straight, but a tear slipped down her cheek. She wiped it away quickly.

"Aw, sweetheart, it's okay. Look, Donner is a police dog and well-behaved. He can come in with me." Wilson said, shooting a look at Nancy.

Nancy raised her hands, "I have no idea if that will work. I'd try it and see how that goes."

Wilson exited the car and opened the back door to let Sarah and Donner out. He looked at Donner. "Walk beside Sarah like you are glued to her side. Sarah, put your hand on him, yes, like that. I'll hold your other hand." He looked at Nancy. "Stay safe," And he closed the back door.

Chapter 9

Finding Sarah

Donner looked around the emergency waiting room. People were sitting and standing everywhere. Halloween is a busy time for hospitals, he mused.

Donner felt Sarah's hand tighten in his fur and leaned closer to her side. Wilson walked up to a wall. "Hello. I am Chief Wilson from Morro Bay. Several people were brought in after an incident on the bay. I'm looking for the Hamptons, Bart, and Eilene Hampton."

Donner heard a voice come from the wall as Sarah's arm encircled his neck. He felt her lay her hand on his head. He heard her whisper, "Let them be okay. Let them be okay." Donner's heart softened, and he yearned to make it less scary for her.

Wilson looked down at Sarah, "Your mom has been admitted. We have permission to go to their room with an escort."

A uniformed man approached the wall. "Hi. I'll take you to the room. Please keep the dog quiet and next to you."

Donner huffed. "I know how to behave, mister security guard."

"Yes, sir," Wilson answered, "Thank you for walking us up there. Sarah is using Donner as a security blanket at the moment. Donner will stay with her."

The man looked down at Sarah, "I see, she is young to be separated from her parents."

"There was chaos at the bay for a while. When things cleared up, we had a crowd of young children to reunite with their parents." Wilson explained as the guard ushered them through a door.

"That's scary, all those children. Are the rest of them okay?" The guard asked as he took them into an elevator.

Wilson nodded, "Yes. The other children's parents were sorted out within an hour, but Sarah's dad came here with her mom. She's been in our care since we identified her. The man her dad left her with needed to be with his wife."

The security guard nodded as the elevator doors opened, and they stepped out. "Oh, good, I was thinking about child endangerment, but she wasn't in danger."

Wilson shook his head, "Nope, although a cat was in danger for a while. Sarah grabbed onto him and wouldn't let go. We finally talked her into hanging with Donner instead."

The man smiled, "I'd sure like to have seen that."

Wilson chuckled, "The cat was in costume, too. He was dressed as Snoopy, who was wearing a pumpkin costume."

The security guard stopped by a door and turned to Wilson. "Remember, no barking, no loose dogs." Then he quietly muttered, "Snoopy costume?" He put his hand to his mouth and shook his head in disbelief. Then he said, "This is the room."

Wilson knocked quietly on the door and pushed it open. Donner and Sarah walked into the room ahead of him. Donner saw a man in a chair beside the bed with his head on the railing. He was looking at the woman on the bed. The woman's eyes were closed. "Bart? Bart Hampton?"

The man turned his head and saw Sarah with Donner. "Sarah? Come here, honey."

Sarah ran to the man and flew into his arms. Donner moved next to Wilson and sat down. Sarah started talking, "Hi, Daddy, how is Mommy? This is Donner. He's a police dog. I was holding Festus, but he couldn't come in. The lady and the gold cat are waiting in the car with Festus."

Bart smiled at Sarah, "You had an adventure, didn't you? I'm glad you are okay." Bart looked at his wife, "Mommy still hasn't woken up. I'm a little worried about her. But I'm better now because I know you are okay." He looked at Wilson, "What happened to Ted?"

Wilson placed his hand on Donner's head. "Sarah didn't feel safe going with Ted, and his wife sprained her ankle pretty badly. Sarah agreed to let me bring her here."

Bart looked at Sarah and shook his head, "Sarah is somewhat of a mystery. We don't know where she got it from, but she is very intelligent. She learned to read last year and knows addition and subtraction."

Sarah sat up, "Don't forget history, geography, and science, Daddy. I love experiments."

Bart shrugged, "She's only three."

Sarah interrupted her daddy, "I'm almost four. My birthday is next month. I saw it on the calendar."

Wilson chuckled, "Yes, Sarah did tell us she is almost four. And that she reads. We enjoyed listening to her." Wilson looked at the woman in the bed. "Bart, what do you plan to do tonight? Will you be allowed to stay in this room with your wife? Should we take Sarah back to Morro Bay tonight? Nancy would enjoy having her."

Bart looked at his wife and then down at Sarah, "I'm not sure. I don't know what to think."

Donner heard a knock at the door, and a voice came from behind him. "Why is there a dog in here?"

Donner leaned heavily on Wilson's leg. "I'm looking for the Hamptons." Wilson stepped aside so the doctor could walk past him. A nurse hurried in after him.

The doctor checked his chart, "It doesn't say anything on here about a dog and a little girl." He looked at the nurse and grinned.

Then the doctor laughed softly, "I'm just kidding. Mr. Hampton, I'm glad you found your little girl. I'm just going to check on your wife now." The doctor moved around the bed, checking instruments, using the rubbery thing around his neck, and shining a light into the woman's eyes. Then he looked at the chart again. "Hmm, there's been no change. She's only on a saline drip at the moment. It says here that she was hit with a paddleboard?"

Bart looked at Wilson and nodded, "Uh, we think that's what happened. There was a large wave, and many people fell off their paddleboards. Eilene didn't come out of the water. I had to go in and get her."

The doctor looked at Wilson, "Morro Bay, Halloween, right, the witch thing. Okay, the thing is, we can't have you in this room overnight. Another patient is coming from the ER and will use the other bed. You should probably say goodnight and take your daughter home for the night."

Bart nodded at the doctor. He drew in a long breath and let it out slowly. "And you'll call me if anything changes?"

The doctor looked at the nurse. "Yes, we have your information. Double-check with your nurse to make sure. Then I suggest you all go home and rest."

Bart stood up and leaned over the woman in the bed. "Good night, Eilene. You were the best witch out there today. Wake up in the morning so we can take you home. I love you, and Sarah does, too." He kissed the woman, and Sarah patted her mommy's hand.

"Night, night, Mommy. Sweet dreams and sunshines tomorrow." Sarah said.

Bart looked at Wilson, "Could I trouble you for a ride?"

Wilson nodded, "That's why we are here! Let's head out." Donner was relieved when they moved out into the hall. Bart spoke to the nurse and gave her his cellphone number again. And then, the security guard led the way out.

Chapter 10

Meanwhile

Sharon bumped into Julian outside the clinic. "Julian, I thought you were doing your walkabout."

Julian shrugged, "I pulled a body from the bay. I brought it here first. They've called Mark, and he's coming to pick it up."

Sharon nodded, "That's why I'm here. I need to catch Mark about a missing detail or two."

Julian peered at Sharon's face, "What's up?"

Sharon shook her head, "I'll tell you later. I had some troubling news from the Coast Guard. I'm hoping Mark can help me with it."

A van pulled into the clinic parking lot and parked in the loading zone. Mark exited the van and put his hands on his hips, "Julian. Are you trying to move in on my girl?"

Julian raised his hands and said, "Whoa, man, no, no, I wouldn't do that."

Mark laughed, "You wouldn't have a chance. I'm surprised daily that I do. She is quite a catch."

Sharon rolled her eyes. "I'll walk in with you, Mark. Continue your walk, Julian."

"Yes, ma'am," Julian said as he hurried to his vehicle.

Sharon shook her head at Mark, "I can't believe you did that. He's got his eye on my neighbor, Mary." Sharon chuckled, "They are cute together."

Mark put his arm around Sharon and pulled her into the clinic. "So, you just couldn't stay away from me, right?"

Sharon frowned, "I need to ask you some questions about Bart."

Mark's head swiveled toward her, "Bart? What about him?"

Sharon shook her head, "I'll ask you in the van. Later."

Mark nodded and turned to the exhausted woman leaning on the counter. "I'm here to pick up a body?"

"Oh, good, that's the last thing I must do. They are in here." The woman walked toward an exam room. "Just bring back our gurneys so I can lock this place up. I've got kids in aftercare."

Mark nodded and followed after her. "Come along, Sharon, you push one, and I'll push the other."

"Good idea," Sharon said as she smiled at the tired woman. "That will make us faster."

"I'll take the man. You grab that one." Sharon said.

Sharon immediately unlocked the brakes and moved the gurney out of the room toward the front door. She heard Mark following behind her with the other body. At the van, Mark opened the back and jumped in. He held out a backboard, and he and Sharon transferred the two bodies into the back.

Sharon grabbed both gurneys and pulled them back to the door. The woman held the door for her, and she quickly stripped both gurneys of linen and tossed them into a box. Sharon parked them back in the exam room. "Good night. Do you want us to wait for you to lock up?" Sharon called.

"No, I've got it." The woman returned with her jacket and purse on one arm and her keys in her hands. "Thanks, anyway."

Sharon walked out of the clinic and moved back to the van. Mark stood by the open passenger door, "In you go," he said.

The woman hurried down the street, turning the corner and quickly disappearing from view. "Wow," Sharon said, "She really must have been late."

Mark nodded, "It is after six. They normally close at five."

"Right," Sharon said as she climbed into the van and sat. Mark shut the door and moved to the driver's side.

As soon as he closed his door, he turned to Sharon and said, "Okay, what about Bart?"

Sharon frowned, "How well do you know Bart?"

"Not that well. He moved into my building complex just a few weeks ago. I was surprised his wife even entered the paddleboard contest. She must be quite the extrovert. Bart isn't," Mark said.

"The Harbor Master and the Coast Guard Coxswain Smith filled me in on the boats on the bay. Four men were on the boat that crashed, but they only pulled out three alive. One of the men said it was Bart's fault. If he'd have been there, everything would have gone smoothly." Sharon read from her notes.

Mark blew out a breath, "That's damning. Meaning he is involved with them. You should text the Chief. He was taking Bart's daughter to the hospital to find her parents. He might want to know."

Sharon took out her phone and started typing a message. "This is crazy. I wonder how he got involved? Maybe that's why they moved here?"

Mark shook his head, "I don't know. I won't be home until after ten tonight, working on these two."

"You're going to start the autopsies?" Sharon asked.

"No, no, just do the preliminary check-in procedure and put them away in the drawers."

Mark started the van. "Are you really leaving your vehicle here?"

"My vehicle is at home. I'll probably check on Jane at the station and then head out." Sharon said.

Mark shook his head, "It looks like we lost one of the paddleboarders and one of the boaters. Not quite the way I wanted to end the day," he said.

"Right. Not like they wanted it either." Sharon mused. "The mayor will not be happy with the publicity from this event. Not family friendly."

"Nope," Mark said as he pulled into the station.

"Do you want some help?" Sharon asked.

"I'm good. You check on Jane. She's still new." Mark said.

Chapter 11

Jane and Susie

When Sharon entered the station, Jane looked up, "Checking up on me, boss?"

Sharon laughed, "Just checking in before I head home. You are still new here. I thought I'd let you ask questions if you had any."

Jane shook her head, "Susie and I are monitoring the Morro Watch and the cameras in this place. The state police came to pick up the three the Coast Guard arrested about an hour ago. Julian checks in every thirty minutes by text. Other than that, it's a quiet night."

Sharon shook her head, "Finally quiet. Mark is putting away two bodies that he will autopsy tomorrow."

Jane nodded, "I saw him wheel in two bodies. It's hard to deal with that sort of thing in such a small community."

Sharon leaned on the counter. "How are you doing with everything here?"

Jane sighed, "I'm sure you've read my file from my last position."

"I did read it, but being a woman police officer, I know it's not usually black and white," Sharon said.

Jane rolled her eyes, "No. But there was a lot of very dark purple involved."

Sharon wrinkled her forehead, "Purple?"

"Never mind," Jane waved away the words, "It was one of those he said she said situations. He had been there longer. Susie hadn't ever liked him, and she protected me. And I don't apologize for that."

Sharon's eyebrows went up, "I see. Then I'm glad Susie has joined the force." Sharon leaned in, "Does she get along with Donner?"

Jane smiled, "There could be too close a relationship there. But in an emergency, both dogs saved people and kept kids safe. I think they work well together."

Sharon grinned, "That's good to hear. It seems like Donner and Festus have built up an animal watch. The seagulls spread messages all over town."

Jane shook her head and frowned at the computer, "I do know they spend time with cats, which is a first for Susie. She's never been a cat-loving dog."

"What's wrong?" Sharon asked.

Jane shook her head, "A weird text from Julian and one of the other watchers." Jane looked up and called to Susie, "Susie, head outside and check with the owl."

Susie jumped up and pushed open the door, trotting across the street and stopping beneath a tree.

Sharon gaped at Jane, "Owl?"

Jane glanced at Sharon, "I'm not crazy, but Wilson said an owl is in the tree. If something is up, the owl will know."

Sharon nodded slowly, "Okay. How will you know if something's going on?"

Just then, Susie raced across the street and jumped on the door. She barked three times and then ran away.

Jane had been typing furiously on the keyboard, and then she sighed. "Okay, Julian says he can handle it. He has some helpers there, and the Coast Guard officers had been taking a dinner break. The watcher said Things are settling down."

Sharon scoffed, "What was it?"

Jane grinned, "Several things at once. A man knelt on the boardwalk to propose, and at the same time, a mother realized she couldn't find her daughter. A group of men tried to leave the restaurant after the couple and made rude comments. One of the guys in front tried to hold his friends back and got punched for the effort."

Sharon relaxed against the counter. "Only in Morro Bay. Wow. Is the little girl okay?"

"Julian sent me a picture. Here, look." Jane turned the screen toward Sharon.

A darling girl dressed in pink and yellow stood looking up at several seagulls. The seagulls were acting surprisingly calm. Nearby were a couple of dogs on either side of her. A sea otter could be seen in the water below her.

Sharon shook her head, "Does it look like two dogs are guarding her from both sides, the seagulls are distracting her, and the sea otter is watching in case she falls in?"

Jane laughed, "It does, doesn't it? Julian said the mother stared at the animals and then led her girl away. The animals dispersed at that moment as if they were done."

They heard the front door thud, "Looks like Susie is back."

Sharon laughed, "She makes herself known. I'll let her in." Sharon walked to the front door and let Susie in. "I'm going to head home and get some sleep before the next emergency." And she walked out the door.

Jane looked down at Susie. "Everything's good? Yeah, that's what Julian said. Go get a drink and a bite to eat." She rubbed Susie's head and then went back to her screens. Susie walked over to her bowls, set out of the way.

Chapter 12

Wilson talks with Bart

Wilson looked up from his phone and turned slightly in his sleep to look at Bart. Sarah lies in his arms with Donner's head in her lap. Festus moves slightly away from My Precious, but she snuggles closer to him. Bart stares into the distance. "Bart? Tell me about the men on that boat."

Bart looks at Wilson in shock, but what he sees in Wilson's eyes causes him to wince. He sighs deeply, causing Sarah to stir. Donner opens his eyes to watch Wilson. "One of the guys talked then. I figured they would. I've been so worried about Eilene that I had forgotten the boat chase."

Bart looks out the window, "I thought I could escape the gang by moving to Morro Bay. Over in Ventura, I didn't see any way to get free. I grew up with them. We've been friends since middle school. One night, Joe was flush with money and spending it freely. After a few drinks, we all demanded to know what was up."

He shook his head, "Joe never was very concerned about right and wrong. He cheated more than he studied. He lied to get girls. I guess it was just a matter of time. He'd done a favor for some new neighbors, and they paid him huge bucks. So, he became a regular with them."

"Sam looked worried, but he usually did whatever Joe told him. Jorge was Joe's best friend. The next thing we knew, we were deep into this new gang. Smuggling drugs, people, guns, even electronics, nothing was excluded. I wanted out, but Joe told me that was impossible. No one leaves the gang."

Bart looked at his little girl. "Sarah had just turned two and surprised us with everything she knew. She could read, and she did, everything she could find. And one time, she saw a list I was given."

Bart's breath hitched, and he swallowed hard. "She held up the paper and asked what it meant. I told her it was a shopping list. She shook her head. That's impossible, she said. We can't afford these things. Are you stealing them?"

"That day, I decided to quit the gang. Eilene and I hadn't renewed our lease and would have to move. Eilene gave away most of our stuff. We kept the sleeper couch, Sarah's bed, and other things, but everything else was gone.

Then we packed our suitcases and drove here to Morro Bay. The Harbor Master immediately found me a job on a boat and helped us get into our apartment. He even gave us some extra furniture he had somewhere. A table and chairs, some dishes, and even a washer-dryer combo." Bart drew in a long breath.

Bart shook his head, "I thought we were safe after a few months. We got new phones and new electronics for Sarah. But somehow, they found me. And they sent my childhood friends to take care of me. They came in on a boat and picked up some things from an old stash.

I told them I couldn't talk until after Halloween. I couldn't ruin Eilene's fun. She was making friends and was happy here. I thought they would just lie low, but they caught sight of another boat in the harbor they could lighten, they said."

"They told you they were going to commit a crime?" Wilson asked.

Bart nodded, "Yes, they did. I knew the people on that boat weren't rich or anything, but they had gotten a contract to help distribute some new-fangled GPS systems. They were selling them in every harbor town from San Diego to north of San Francisco.

So I mentioned their intentions to George, and the Coast Guard watched them. I guess they figured the whole town would be busy with the Halloween Paddle event."

A tear dropped down Bart's cheek and fell on Donner's head. "I didn't think about them trying to escape and causing waves. I really didn't."

Wilson sighed, "Thanks for sharing, Bart." Nancy turned off the highway onto Harbor Street. "Let's get you and Sarah home, Bart. Where's your place?"

Another tear dropped down Bart's cheek as Wilson mumbled, "The same complex where Mark lives."

Nancy nodded, "Then we are almost there, Bart. You'll feel better after some sleep."

Chapter 13

Mary and Julian

Mary set the bag on the table and set out the food containers. "Thank you for eating with me, Julian. I know you are busy with your shift."

Julian grabbed the napkins Mary had laid on the table before they blew away. He put half under his container and half under her container. Then he grabbed the straws before they rolled away and put one in each cup. "I can't thank you enough for getting me food. I'm starving. I always get hungry this time of night, probably because everything is closed."

Mary blushed, and Julian smiled. "Of course," he thought, "it might just be the bracing wind coming ashore with the fog." Aloud, he said, "Are these leftovers from your shift?"

"No!" Mary exclaimed as she grabbed her fork before it flew away. "I ordered these before the cook started cleaning the grill. I thought we deserved some warm food after such a busy day." Mary picked up half a sandwich. "Did you really pull a body from the bay?"

Julian grimaced, "There were two dead bodies. One was a paddleboarder. That was really sad. I missed her the first three times I looked. Then I walked the beach until I found a way to pull her to shore without swimming."

"Did you know her?" Mary asked.

Julian shook his head, "No. But I'm still fairly new here. I don't know everyone yet. It seemed like no one missed her, which is odd. Unless the mayor has gotten a call." Julian shrugged and opened his cup of clam chowder. "Oh, yes, the chowder here is awesome. Doesn't matter which restaurant you go to, it seems."

Mary laughed, "Don't tell my boss that. She thinks that hers is the best. She threw in the soup at the last minute. I only ordered hot sandwiches and beans."

Julian grinned, "She knows I always order the chowder whenever I go in there. It's just I do that in all the other restaurants, too."

"Aren't you tired of it yet?" Mary asked.

"You would think so, but each chowder is slightly different. And I think it is slimming. I've been losing weight. My pants are loose at the waist." Julian leaned forward and winked.

Mary giggled. "Still, what do you do for variety?"

"Eating with you is different. Makes me think I'm having the best food with the best company." Julian said. Just then, the lid to the soup flew away. "Rats. Now I've littered. I'll have to hunt that down and put it in the trash."

Mary watched a seagull swoop to the ground, pick up the lid, and drop it into the trash can. "I think that bird just did it for you."

"What?" Julian's head turned away, "I didn't see anything. Are you teasing me? Seagulls don't pick up trash. They pull it from the trash and throw it on the ground."

Mary scrunched her forehead and nose, "I know what I saw. That bird flew down, picked up the lid, flew to the top of the trash can, and dropped the lid in."

"That's ridiculous. I tell you, that's not how it goes." He turned toward the trash can and put his soup on his lips. "I'll watch while I eat my soup. You'll see."

Then, a seagull landed a few feet from their table. The bird walked under a table, further from the building. It picked up a container with its beak and awkwardly flew to the trash can. The container dangled above the trash can, and the seagull dropped it inside. Then it sat on the can and stared at them.

Julian slowly set down his cup and looked at Mary, "Did you see that? It's like the seagull was listening to me and wanted to prove me wrong!"

Mary's eyes were huge as she said, "This isn't going to be like that Hitchcock movie about birds, is it? They aren't going to attack?"

Julian turned back to Mary and shook his head, "Naw. That won't happen. Well, it did sort of happen to Noah. He was checking a lead on a disturbance, and some guy jumped out of the shadows with a gun. A bunch of seagulls dive-bombed the guy and pooped all over him. The guy dropped the gun and started crying. It took Noah weeks to get the bird poop out of his car."

When he looked up, Mary was staring at him. "That did not happen, did it? Tell me it didn't."

Julian nodded, "It did happen. I didn't see it. But the animals around here seem organized. It's like they patrol the town like I do."

Mary looked at Julian, "I think you are making this all up."

"How can you say that? After what we just saw that seagull do?" Julian asked.

Mary laughed, "Fine. Be that way." She tightly pulled her jacket around her, "It's cold out here. I think I need to go home."

"Did you finish eating?" Julian asked.

Mary shook her head, "No. But I'm done with food for a while. I need to get some sleep so I can work in the morning."

Julian stood up, grabbed the bag from Mary, stuffed everything into it, and tossed it into the trash can. "Okay, I'll walk you home."

Mary shook her head, "You don't need to do that. I don't want to take you from your job."

"Walking the streets is my job, Mary. I'll see you to your door." Julian said as he took her arm.

Mary ducked her head, "Okay." She slung her bag so it hung in front of her, and she fell into step with Julian. "Thank you."

"Thank you, Mary," Julian said as he glanced around. "Feels like we are being watched. I'll feel better when you are home safe."

Mary and Julian walked away quickly, crossing the street and moving up the hill. Behind him sat a line of seagulls on the roof of the restaurant. "He's pretty sharp, that one. He figured we were watching him."

"Doofus. He doesn't know it's us. He doesn't care about birds," said the one beside him.

Then, a shadow separated from the side of the building and made its way across the street, following Julian and Mary.

"That, Doofus, is what he was feeling. And since you had so much fun with him tonight, you can follow Julian around just in case he gets in trouble. Off you go."

"That's pronounced Dohfoo, thank you very much. I thought I was off work, Cecil," Doofus complained.

"Move it," Cecil commanded as he sniped at Doofus.

"Okay, okay," cried Doofus.

Cecil turned to look at the other birds. "Who wants to report to Donner?" All the birds stayed silent. "George, you head out with Doofus and follow the man behind Julian. I want to know where he is going. The rest of you keep watch. I'll be at Donner's place."

One seagull said, "I thought the Chief had gone to the hospital?"

"He just got home. Did you see that?" Cecil sighed, "Pay attention, birds. At least one of you." Then Cecil flew off to find Donner and report.

Chapter 14

Noah and Olivia at his place

Olivia looked up from the book she was reading. Yes, she did hear Noah moving around. Olivia hurried to the microwave to reheat the tea inside. Then she walked the cup into his bedroom. Noah muttered in his sleep and wrestled with his blankets.

Setting down the cup on the side table, Olivia spoke softly, "Noah, it's okay, Noah." When he didn't quit, she raised her voice until the command was clear, "Noah, wake up, now."

Noah jerked and lay still. He slowly opened his eyes and groaned, "My head, why did you wake me up?"

Olivia picked up the cup and sat on the bed next to Noah. "Sit up and drink a little of this tea. It's good for headaches."

Noah shoved himself up a little, and Olivia held the cup to his lips, "I'm not an invalid, you know."

Olivia chuckled, "I know. But tonight I am the boss of you." Noah took a sip and slurped some more, nearly draining the cup. Olivia sat back. "You were having a nightmare."

Noah grimaced, "I drank the tea. Can I go back to sleep now?"

Olivia pulled out the little flashlight and quickly checked Noah's pupils. "Hmm, still even. If you don't want to talk about why you were thrashing around on the bed, then sure, go back to sleep."

Olivia stood, and Noah grabbed her arm to stop her. "I was back in the water again, trying to save people, but all I did was get shoved and hit by bodies and boards. I couldn't see, and I couldn't breathe because I was under the water. I didn't know which way was up. I panicked."

Olivia nodded, "That's understandable. It sounds horrible. You can't protect yourself for fear you might hurt someone."

Noah relaxed a little, "You understand."

Olivia nodded. "It was a mass casualty emergency. Some people were seriously hurt. Most of them went to the hospital. But not you. Instead, you got me to watch over you. But I understand. We only lost one boarder in all that mess, thank God."

"Still," Noah said, "We did lose one. What about the woman I was next to? It wasn't her, was it?"

Olivia shook her head, "No, her name is Eilene, and she is in the hospital. As far as I know, she hasn't regained consciousness."

"Wait, Eilene? Married to Bart? A little girl named Sarah?" Noah asked.

Olivia stared at him, "You know them?"

"I see Eilene and Sarah at the park a lot. Sarah likes to talk to me and ask questions. She has a thirsty brain. That's what I tell her." Noah's smile was small and brief.

"What's in that tea you are giving me?" he asked.

"It's Chamomile plus a little Wild Lettuce and Tumeric." Olivia said, "My mom uses it at home."

"Wild Lettuce? Turmeric, I've heard of, but Wild Lettuce? You're making that up." Noah said.

"No. It's a blend my mom makes at home. She sells it online." Olivia's eyes flashed at Noah.

"Oh. Sorry." Noah said. "I hope Eilene wakes up. She's good with Sarah."

"We'll know more in the morning. The chief made it home with Bart and Sarah. He's probably sleeping by now." Olivia said. "Something you should get back to."

Olivia stood and picked up the empty cup. "I'll make another cup so it's ready for you in a few hours."

"Thank you, Olivia. I really hate hospitals. So, thanks for taking care of me so I could come home." Noah said.

"Anytime, big guy. Your apartment is nice." Olivia said as she walked out. She refilled the cup with tea from the pot and then placed it in the microwave.

Then, she sat down on the recliner and picked up the book. But she didn't read it. She stared out the window and watched the wind blow.

Chapter 15

Festus Types

"I can't believe you got me up so early. I'm still wearing my pajamas." Festus said. "Pete will wonder where I am."

Donner huffed, "He'll just call Wilson, and Wilson will find us. Keep typing."

"Yeah, yeah, how much more is there to tell?" Festus grumbled as his tail collided again with the tail of his pajamas.

"What are you supposed to be in that get-up?" Donner asked.

Festus glared at him, "A lion, of course. Okay, what about the guy that, did you say, Doofus? Was following?"

"Right. Julian went down the hill to Main Street and walked along the businesses there. He was checking doors and listening in the alleys."

Donner said, "And the guy was following Julian. He may still be doing it. At some point, Julian arrived at the station to check in with Jane, and Susie ran out the door when Julian opened it."

"Susie chased the guy?" Festus asked.

"Yep. She could smell him behind Julian and raced out. The man took off running, slipped into a vehicle, and then drove away." Donner said. "But no license plate. Apparently, Doofus isn't good at numbers."

Festus mumbled, "Who is?"

Wilson's phone rang in the bedroom, and Festus looked at Donner. Then he started typing faster. "I'm going, I'm going, I've nearly got it."

Wilson stumbled into the living room and stared at Donner and Festus. He mumbled into the phone, "Yeah, he's here. I'll send him home." Wilson scrubbed his face, "I need more sleep. Am I going to get any? You make a cute lion, Festus. Roar."

Festus looked at Donner and shook his head. Wilson collapsed in his recliner, and Festus jumped into his lap with the tablet. "Thanks, Festus. I appreciate your hard work. Thanks, Donner. Can you walk Festus home?"

Wilson turned to the tablet and yawned. Donner and Festus left through the doggie door. Festus's tail caused the lion costume's tail to waggle back and forth. Donner rolled his eyes.

Festus yawned. "I hope I can sleep in the next costume. I need a nap."

"I agree with you there. I have no idea what's going to happen today." Donner said.

"Well, Mark will do the autopsies and write his report, Wilson will get a report from the state police on the boater gang, and he'll need to check in with Nancy and Sharon. And Julian, too." Festus finished his litany of tasks, and Donner groaned.

"I will sleep later, I guess," Donner said.

"Home!" Festus shouted and dived into the cat door. Then he stuck his head out, "See ya later, Donner."

Donner turned to head back home but stopped in his tracks. A bulldog stood in his way. "Hey, Shaun. How's it hanging?" Donner said.

Shaun continued to stare at Donner. Then, a seagull landed on Shaun's head, "Get out of here, Shaun. Don't mess with Donner."

Donner watched Shaun slink away and turned back to Cecil. "You were busy last night."

"Yes, I was. Too busy. I need a second in command. I'm too old to fly all over town." Cecil squawked. "I have no idea who I have that's smart and brave enough and with common sense. That's not a common combination in seagulls."

"What about a smaller land bird or an owl?" Donner asked.

"No self-respecting seagull would take orders from a land bird. An owl, maybe." He nodded, "I'll think about that. Thanks, Donner."

"Did you have more to report, Cecil?" Donner asked.

"Oh, yeah. The guy who followed Julian last night is parked in front of Sharon's house." Cecil said.

Donner stared at him, "Is he being watched?"

"Yes, a couple of neighbor dogs are sitting outside his car." Cecil chuckled, "He's scared to get out of his car."

Donner turned to the cat door, sticking his head into Pete's house. "Festus, I need you to do some typing for me. It's urgent."

Festus ran into the room for the door, "Move out of the way! He's got a beachball!"

Donner pulled his head out, and Festus jumped through the door. Donner had to hurry to catch up with him. "What's this about a beachball?" Donner panted.

Festus slowed his pace, "The new...costume...is a beachball. I can't sleep in that. I'm not going home until I get some sleep."

Donner's eyes widened, and he huffed a few times. "Wow, okay, well, we need Wilson. I hope he's still home."

Donner filled Festus in as they ran up to the doggie door. When Donner landed inside, Wilson was snoring in his chair. The tablet was on his lap. Festus jumped onto the chair and started typing.

"Okay, Donner, I'm done. Wake him up." Festus said as he jumped to the floor.

Donner barked twice sharply. Wilson jerked awake. He looked at Donner and then Festus, "Where's your costume, Festus? Did you go home?"

Donner barked again, louder this time. Wilson and Festus covered their ears. "Donner, what's up?" Wilson's hand came down on the tablet, and he looked at it. "There's more."

Wilson picked up the tablet and read silently for a few minutes. Then he shook his head and checked for his phone. Donner pointed at the table next to him. "Oh, there it is, thanks, Donner."

"Jane? Are you still at the station? Is Julian there?" Wilson yawned through the words.

"Yes, I'm here. I'm not sure where Susie is, but I'm here. I've got another hour on my shift." Jane said. "Why, what's up?"

Donner heard Jane yell Julian's name. Wilson pulled the phone away from his ear, "Ouch."

"Sorry, Chief. I'm not that coordinated this late in a night shift." Jane said. "Here's Julian."

"Yeah, Chief, what's up?" Julian asked.

"Did you notice a man following you last night when you walked Mary home?" Wilson asked.

"How did you know I...? Never mind, no, Mary and I both felt like someone was watching us. Mary thought it was the seagulls. Who was he?" Julian asked.

"He's parked in front of Mary's house right now, guarded by two dogs. He can't get out of his car." Wilson said.

"I'm on my way," Julian said, and Wilson pulled the phone from his head again, "Ouch."

"Sorry, Chief," Julian threw the phone on the counter and ran out the door. What's going on?" Jane asked.

"Just some guy parked in front of Mary's house after following Julian to the station last night," Wilson said.

"Oh," Jane said. "Wow."

"I'll be in there in an hour. If Denny comes in, have him wait for me." Wilson said.

"Okay. Who's Denny?" Jane asked.

"He's ready for light duty and will take over the desk this morning. He's an officer injured in the line of duty." Wilson said.

"Oh, okay. I'll keep an eye out for him and try to show him the setup or answer questions." Jane said.

"Thanks, Jane. Get some sleep today. Susie is probably one of the dogs at Mary's house. Across from Sharon's place." Wilson said.

"Got it. Thanks." Jane hung up.

Wilson looked around the room. Donner and Festus were lying on the rug, fast asleep. Wilson groaned. He looked at the clock, "Thirty more minutes," and promptly snored.

Chapter 16

Mary's House

Susie barked at the man again and lunged at the door, knocking it shut again. The man cried out in frustration. Susie growled at him. "How long do we have to keep this up, Susie. I'm tired." Said the other dog.

"Don't you move from the car, Petey. Keep barking. It's not like I had any sleep either." Susie barked loudly.

Petey jumped at the window and barked when the man slid into the passenger seat. "Come on, someone has to help me. No one can sleep through this!" the man said.

Susie kept her barks sharp and loud even as she heard Julian running down the street. "Julian is almost here, Petey. As soon as he arrives, you can go home. Thanks for your help." Susie barked.

She heard Petey mutter, "Last time I fall for the romantic line. At least my doghouse was cozy." He barked and jumped at the car again.

Julian ran to the side of the car next to Susie. "It's okay, girl. I've got this." Julian said. He looked into the car at the man opening the door and raced to the other side. "Hello, sorry about that. Do you live around here?"

The man straightened and looked up at Julian. "No, I came down to surprise my girlfriend. I was just sitting here quietly in the car, waiting for daylight," the man said.

"Yes? And your name, sir? For my report, you see." Julian whipped out his notepad and pen as he blocked the man's way.

"Sure. Mike Johnson. I live in San Luis near the college." Mike said.

"I see." Julian scrutinized him. "Are you a professor there?"

Mike nodded, "Well, I teach there. I'm an assistant to a professor while I finish my PhD. I'm slated to join the staff next year."

Julian nodded, "That's great. It takes a lot of work to get a PhD." Julian looked at the houses on the street, "Where does your girlfriend live?"

Mike pointed at Mary's house, and Julian frowned. He thought to himself, "She didn't mention a boyfriend or where she came from." Out loud, he said, "And you come down often at the end of a weekend?"

Mike attempted to close his door to move past Julian, but Julian stood on his ground. "No, not usually. I was worried about her. She hasn't returned my calls and texts."

A car turned down the street and parked in front of Mike's car. Julian kept his eye on Mike while Wilson exited the vehicle. "How long has it been since you spoke to her?" he asked Mike.

Wilson walked around the cars and patted Susie on the head. Julian heard him whisper, "Good girl. Head back to Jane now." Then Susie moved from the cars toward the station but stopped to watch.

Wilson walked around the cars to stand next to Julian. "I believe this officer asked you a question, sir. I'd like to hear the answer."

Mike stuttered and finally muttered, "It's been a few months."

"Interesting, uh," Wilson began.

"Mike Johnson," Julian provided.

"That's interesting, Mike, that you seem so concerned about her, but are you just now checking up on her in person?" Wilson said.

He glanced at Julian, "And it seems that someone who answers to your description was spotted following Julian here earlier tonight.

You followed him on foot all the way to the station, didn't you? Where did you pick up this car?"

Julian stared at Wilson, then turned to Mike. "What? Why were you following me?"

Mike glared at Wilson and Julian. "So what if I followed him? That's not against the law, is it?"

Wilson sighed, "Actually, it is against the law. Julian is a police officer on duty performing his walkabout. The only reason to follow a police officer is to see where he goes. It makes you look very guilty, Mike."

"I don't believe this! Okay, he was out with my girl, eating with her. And then he walked her home. I didn't like it." Mike said, his fists curled tight.

"You think he should have let a young woman walk home in the dark late at night, do you?" Wilson shook his head, "That's not how I would feel if it were my girl."

"Why don't we get Mary out here so she can vouch for you, Mike?" Wilson said as he stepped away from the car and moved down the sidewalk.

Julian felt Mike tense next to him and grabbed his arm just as Mike crouched to get back in the car. "No, I don't think you should leave yet, Mike. Stay right where you are."

Mike nearly growled, and an answering growl came from behind Julian. "Keep that dog away from me. She should be put down."

Susie barked, and Mike shrank back toward the car. Julian heard Mary's soft voice and Wilson's deep rumble. Then Wilson came back to the car as Mary shut the door. Wilson pulled out his handcuffs as he walked, and Mike groaned. "I don't need this."

"You brought it on yourself, Mike. Apparently, there is a restraining order on you, and you are breaking it right now. Julian read him his rights." Wilson said.

Wilson put the handcuffs on Mike while Julian began, "You have the right to be silent..."

Chapter 17

Eilene's Tasks

At the hospital, the nurse glanced at the alarm and ran down the hall. When she reached the room, her patient climbed into sweatpants. She marched into the room with purpose, "What are you doing out of bed? After your husband sat here half the night worrying about you?" She put her hands on her hips. "Get back in bed right now!"

Eilene turned to the nurse and stared, "But, Sarah,"

"No buts," the nurse stated as she guided Eilene under the sheet. "You were unconscious for over 12 hours. You have a concussion and have to be cleared by a doctor."

"It's just, Sarah," Eilene began again.

"Was here with her daddy at the end. She was worried about you, too, but was tired. The police chief brought her in with his dog. The nerve of that man! A dog on my floor." The nurse glanced at her watch, "The shift change is in thirty minutes, and I will be busy talking to my replacement. You will stay in that bed until the doctor comes to examine you."

She quickly replaced the wires and tubes, shaking her head at the IV. "I'll have to call someone about this." Then she walked out the door.

Eilene stared after her and wondered if she should get up again. She had been dizzy. She thought about Bart and Sarah and looked for a phone. There didn't seem to be one. Then, another nurse walked into the room, reading the chart. "Well, let's see how you're doing, Eilene."

She looked up when she nearly tripped over Eilene's shoes on the floor. "Oh, you're awake! Oh, my, you took out your IV. Ouch, that had to hurt." She looked down at the shoes and back at Eilene, "Were you trying to escape? Oh, dear, that's not good. We get in trouble for that."

Eilene said, "But Sarah,"

"Honey, I met Sarah last night. She is an amazing little girl. You are doing a great job with her. So polite and sweet, even if she is smarter than most people." The nurse made notes on the chart and bustled around the room. "Here it is. Let me put this by the bed for you."

Eilene smiled as the nurse placed the phone on her tray and moved it closer to her. "Dial nine to get an outside line, then the area code first. And I'll be back in ten." She bustled out the door as Eilene picked up the phone.

Sarah answered on the first ring. "Is this you, Momma? It says San Luis on the phone."

"Yes, baby, it's me. Are you doing okay?" Eilene smiled.

"I'm good, Momma. Daddy is still asleep. He was very worried about you, I could tell. But the doctor said you should wake up soon. We got home really late.

I got to hold Snoopy. Well, he wasn't a dog; he was a cat in a dog costume named Festus. He types. And then I held onto a real police dog, Donner. He is very big.

Then Wilson and the Hobbit, named Nancy, drove me to see you and Daddy. Then they brought Daddy and me back home. Wasn't that nice?" Sarah rattled on.

"Sarah, you aren't going to do your regular schedule today, you know? Daddy doesn't know everything to do." Eilene said.

"But you have a list, Momma. It's on the re- frigerator. I think Daddy can follow the list." Sarah announced.

"I know he can, sweetie, but he might have to work. I'll know more about my schedule after the doctor examines me again this morning. I don't know when that is. If he has to work, you can stay with our neighbor. Her number..." Eilene said.

"It's on the refrigerator. I know, Momma. I'd rather hang out with Wilson again, but I can take extra books." Sarah sighed heavily.

"Have your daddy call me when he wakes up, okay, Sarah?" Eilene asked.

"Yes, mommy, I will. And I'll be a good girl until he wakes up. As you said, I ate my breakfast already, one of the ready-made boxes in the refrigerator. I can have one of the snacks in the pantry next and drink water." Sarah said.

"Thank you, Sarah. I feel much better now. I love you." Eilene said.

"I love you, Mommy," Sarah said.

Eilene disconnected as the nurse entered the room. "Did you talk to your husband?" she asked.

Eilene shook her head and winced, "No. He's asleep. I talked to my daughter. She is handling everything okay."

"You are a capable mother, and she is a capable girl. She's safe. Good, now, I'll take your vitals and let you nap until breakfast. I ordered toast, juice, and oatmeal for you." The nurse said as she checked the readings and wrote them on the chart.

Eilene closed her eyes and smiled. "Sarah is safe for now. I can rest." Then she fell asleep.

The nurse finished the charts and walked out the door. The charge nurse stood outside and glared at her. "Is she still in bed?"

The nurse grinned, "I let her use the phone, and now that she knows her daughter is safe, she is sleeping."

"Oh, I see. You'll have to wait until the doctor comes to reinsert the IV. He may decide against it." She turned around and tossed her

parting words over her shoulder, "Ten minutes until shift change."

Chapter 18

Denny's Return

When Sharon walked in the front door, Denny was staring at the computer on the front counter. "Good morning, Denny. How's it going?" she said.

"Morning, Sharon. You didn't get much rest last night." Denny said, "Jane gave me a rundown of the Morro Watch and what to look for before she left. Her dog showed up here as she was walking out the door."

"Good. Now that you've spent time with it, do you have any questions?" Sharon leaned on the counter and waited for Denny's reply.

Denny grimaced, "I get how everything works. So, most of the town knows nothing about the Watch?"

"Nope," Sharon said, "We think it is safer for them that way. To other people, it looks like they are checking social media online."

"Oh, right, safer. That makes sense. So the Harbor Master, George, doesn't know one of his employees is on the Watch?" Denny asked.

"No, he doesn't. He wouldn't like it. He'd think we were spying on him." Sharon said.

"Well, aren't we?" Denny asked.

"It is a kind of surveillance. We have a small group of officers and a big town to cover. The Watch helps us keep an eye on what's happening, a fight starting, or someone committing a crime." Sharon said.

"Yes, that seems like a great idea. But George still wouldn't like it. He's a private kind of guy." Denny said.

Sharon watched Denny for a minute longer, "We are still learning how to use it. No one is guilty without evidence. So we look into things the same as if we had a tip line." She nodded her head, "Is the Chief in?"

Denny nodded, "He just came in a few minutes ago. He and Julian brought in a suspect."

"Okay. Thanks." Sharon said as she walked down the hallway.

Denny looked after her and wondered what George would say about the Watch. "I'm not going to mention it to him, that's for sure." He muttered to himself.

Denny heard Julian as he greeted Sharon in the hallway. Denny turned back to the computer.

"Hey, Denny. Glad to have you back. You're looking good. How are you?" Julian said as he leaned on the counter. "Is there anything happening in town?"

Denny shook his head, "There are lots of messages, but not really anything happening. It just seems like a lot of noise."

Julian frowned, "Do they seem to be all over town or concentrated in one area?" he asked.

"Both!" Denny said and then sighed. "I think I'm getting tired. This is harder than I thought it would be."

Julian pulled a chair up to the counter. "Sit, Denny. Let me check the messages while you relax for a bit. Take a drink. Do you have a drink up here? I'll grab you a drink, bottle of water, or soda?"

Denny sat in the chair and groaned, "I don't know."

Julian ran down the hall and grabbed a bottle of water from the package on the floor. He rushed back to the front and saw Denny slumped in the chair with his eyes shut. "Here, Denny." Julian opened the bottle and handed it to Denny.

Denny opened his eyes and slowly drank from the bottle. When it was half gone, he put it down. Julian put the lid back on. "When did you last eat, Denny? Breakfast?"

Denny shook his head. "I was too nervous to eat this morning. I was worried I'd be late."

Julian checked his Watch, "It's 9 am now. I can still get you breakfast somewhere. What sounds good?"

Denny shook his head, "Nothing." A tear dropped down his cheek.

Julian took a deep breath. "You know, Olivia only worked part-time at first. She did the afternoon shift. That might work better for you."

"I couldn't do that. What would the Chief say?" Denny asked.

"He'd say you need to take care of yourself, Denny, or you can't do your job." Wilson came around the corner, Sharon close behind. Denny groaned again.

Wilson continued, "You went through major trauma. It takes time to get back to full speed. I'll get the papers ready, so your disability can continue. Sharon will fix your schedule."

Wilson started to leave, then turned to Julian, "Scrambled eggs and toast with hashbrowns. Now, Julian, go!"

Julian ran out the front door, and Wilson walked down the hall. Sharon came to the counter and looked at the computer. "Hmm. You've been busy, Denny. Good work."

Denny snuffed, "You really think so?"

Sharon nodded as she began typing. "This system is easy in theory, but it takes a lot of brain power. You used up all of your energy in the first few hours. I'll get Noah to come relieve you. You'll feel better after you eat, but you should have a nap and do some walking. Not policing, mind you, just walking."

When Sharon glanced at Denny, his eyes were closed again. She saw the tear tracks on his cheeks. She turned back to the computer and did some checking. She quietly worked while Denny slept.

Chapter 19

Sharon and Bart

"I need to talk to Bart, question him," Sharon said firmly.

Wilson shook his head, "I told you what he said to me, Sharon. He's not part of that group anymore."

"I need to know who they are working with and get some details," Sharon said again.

"You want to figure it out before the Coast Guard does?" Wilson asked.

Sharon looked at the ceiling, "Are you sure they will do something?"

"They rooted out the corruption in town, Sharon. All of the new people have been vetted over and over. We have our people keeping track of them." Wilson said.

"Something is going on in this town. What Denny handled this morning was an influx of information. But he sorted it out, noting the message type and the location. He did a good job." Sharon said.

"But..." Wilson said.

"But something is going on. I don't know what. I hoped I could figure out some things if I talked to Bart." Sharon said.

"Fine, he should be waking up by now. He's got Sarah with him, so be careful." Wilson said.

"Will do, Chief." Sharon waved as she walked out the door.

She was determined to get information from Bart. It wasn't that far to his place, so she set off on foot. Noah was busy with the computer when she left. He seemed good this morning.

After a quick walk, Sharon walked up the stairs to Bart's apartment. She knocked on the door and was resigned to waiting for an answer. But the door flew open, and the little girl from yesterday stood there staring at her. "Um, hello, I'm Sharon. I'm here to talk to your dad."

Sarah nodded at Sharon and pulled the door open to let her in. "You can sit in the living room. I'll go get him. He just got up."

Sharon sat down on the couch and looked around the tiny space. A tablet sat on the table open to a college course website. She leaned forward to see if she could read it, but it blinked off.

Sarah came back into the room and picked up the tablet. She sat on the floor and leaned on a chair. "He's coming."

Then she turned back to her tablet, engrossed in the content. Sharon couldn't see any pictures on the page. She cleared her throat, "What are you reading?"

Sarah looked up at her, "I'm supposed to be working on my literature class. Momma wants me to be well-rounded, but I sneak in lectures from the Physics course. It's more interesting."

"Oh, okay," Sharon said.

Bart entered the living room and sat on the chair beside the couch. He patted Sarah's head. "Hello. You're Sharon, right? You visit Mark."

Sharon nodded, "Yes, that's right. I wanted to ask you a few questions about those men from yesterday."

Bart nodded, "Yes. The nicest one is the one who drowned. He was my friend for a long time."

Sharon sighed, "I'm sorry to hear that. That's tough."

Bart sat back in the chair, "Especially since I told the Coast Guard to watch them. It's like I'm responsible for what happened." He looked at Sharon with tears in his eyes, "I didn't want anyone to get hurt."

Sharon nodded, "I understand, Bart. Tell me, did you know anything about the men your friends were working for?"

"Bad news, very bad news. I think they were from out of town, out of the country, but not from Mexico." Bart said. "As soon as the guys were approached by them, I cut ties with them all. I'd been involved in a gang a long time ago. I didn't want to do that again. So Eilene and I left town and everyone behind us."

Sharon looked at Sarah and saw her watching Bart. She looked at Bart, "Is it okay to talk in front of Sarah?"

Bart nodded, "Oh, yes. She's the one who told me to leave them all. She got her mom on her side, and I couldn't resist them."

Sarah put her tablet down, "I may look young, but I understand adult things. It wasn't safe for my daddy or Momma at our old place. This place is safer."

Sarah climbed on Bart's lap and hugged his neck. "Oh, Momma called this morning, Daddy."

Bart looked at her, "She's awake?"

Sarah laughed, "Duh! How else could she call me?" Sarah giggled like the little girl she was, and Sharon smiled. "She'll call again after she sees the doctor."

Bart smiled and relaxed some, "She'll call again. That's great news!" He hugged Sarah.

He looked at the tablet, "Is that a Physics lecture? You know what your Momma said."

Sarah looked at her daddy, "Well, Momma isn't here, so I'm getting a little treat for myself."

Bart shook his head, "Okay, but make sure you are caught up with your other reading, or I'll get in trouble."

Sarah grinned. "I'll finish it, Daddy. I only have a hundred pages left. It was just boring."

Sharon felt her eyes grow big. "Wow," she mouthed.

Bart looked at Sharon. "Would you like some coffee? I need to eat. Then Sarah and I will go to the hospital to see Momma."

Sharon shook her head, "No coffee for me. I had a good breakfast a few hours ago. I need to go, but if you think of any details to help me identify those men, that would be great."

"The Coast Guard didn't get anything from my friends?" Bart frowned. "They need to talk and get away with their families."

"I'm not sure what the Coast Guard has. They aren't sharing. But one of the men mentioned you, so I told them I would check you out.

Hopefully, they won't try to talk to you them-selves." Sharon shrugged, "You really weren't involved with them, were you?"

Bart shook his head, "No. When they came into town and went to my work, they tried to loop me in. But I stood firm. I was done with that life. I might not be rich, but I'm on the right side of the law."

Sharon watched Bart straighten his back. She found herself liking him. "Just let Mark know if you need to talk to me. We talk several times a day. I want to know if anything is troubling you. Or if you see anything that isn't right. Okay?" Sharon held out her hand, and Bart shook it.

"Yes, ma'am. I will do that. I'll do my part in protecting this town." Bart stated.

Chapter 20

Mary Drops By

Wilson watched Mary in the chair in front of his desk. He liked Mary, but he was worried about his officer. "Mike is an ex-boyfriend, is that correct?"

Mary nodded. "Yes, sir. We went out on two dates, but I didn't like how he treated the waitstaff. It bothered me how rude he was to them."

"How did Mike take the breakup?" Wilson asked.

Mary looked at her hands clasped in her lap. "He didn't like it at all. Mike told me I couldn't break up with him. He'd kill anyone else I dared to date. So.."

"Yes?" Wilson said. Donner got up from his place by the wall and walked over to Mary's chair. He put his head on her lap.

Mary sighed and rubbed Donner's head. She looked up at Wilson and raised her chin. "I told my employer I could do my work at home. He agreed to let me do that, and then I packed what I could in my car. Then I drove here and found a place to rent."

Wilson shook his head and asked, "How do you think he found you?"

"I don't know, sir." Mary said, "I gave my electronics to a homeless person and bought new ones before leaving town. Fortunately, I had some savings built up."

"That's why you have that old car you drive. You traded in your previous car." Wilson nodded. "That's pretty smart. But it leaves us with the question, how did he find you?"

Mary sat silently while she rubbed Donner's head. "I've always gotten my mail at a post office box rather than at my place. I've moved too much in the last decade, and it was just easier."

"Does the post office forward your mail?" Wilson asked.

"It's actually just a box set up in a store. The owner is a coarse man who is a stickler for rules. He gave me one key and told me not to let anyone else have it for any reason. So I keep it on a different keychain than my home and car." Mary said slowly.

"Does he know about Mike?" Wilson asked.

"Yes, he does. He told me he didn't like him and to stay away from Mike." Mary smiled, "So when I left town, I told him what I was going to do. He thought that was a great idea, just to make sure my new place was close to a police officer."

"And you found a place across the street from Sharon. Nice." Wilson said. "What does he do with your mail?"

Mary laughed, "He ships it in a box through the mail, but he addresses it to Marvin Gladstone. That way, nothing leaves his place with my name visible."

Wilson's eyes sparkled, "Hmm. Same initials as you. Mary Garcia."

"Yes. I thought it was very clever of him. Plus, he stuck the junk mail in my box in case anyone checks it." Mary smiled. "I felt like I had someone on my side. Even if he was a gruff old man."

Wilson nodded, "Those are the best kind. They can be true friends."

Mary shook her head, "I just don't know how he found me, Mike, I mean."

"We'll keep looking for a connection. Sometimes it takes luck, but usually it's just turning over every rock in sight." Wilson said. "I'll let Sharon know about Mike as well as Mark. They might hear something or stumble across a clue."

Mary nodded. "Thank you, sir."

Wilson winced, "Just call me Wilson, Mary. That works fine. I'm actually retired, you know." Donner raised his head and looked at Wilson as he huffed.

Mary giggled, "It sounds like Donner doesn't agree with you."

Wilson stood, "We both liked it better when we were retired. But we have to find the right fit this time. We need someone who loves this town as much as the rest of us do. And has honesty, integrity, and staying power."

Mary's eyes widened, "That's a tall order, sir, uh, Wilson. How are we going to find someone like that? It would take a miracle."

Wilson looked her straight in the eyes, "Yes. That's right. It will take a miracle. I can hardly wait to see how it works out."

Donner barked as Mary stood. "Here now, Donner, don't startle her. I'll walk you to the front."

He and Mary walked down the hall with Donner following close behind them. The smell of pizza wafted toward them, "Hmm." Wilson said, breathing deeply. "Noah is in the house. That smells good."

Chapter 21

Joe and Mike

Mike slumped in the corner of the cell while he waited for someone to bail him out. Joe wasn't going to like this. Joe had ordered him to stay away from Mary. But he couldn't help it. He thought, Mary is mine!

Mike saw Julian walk by the hall door, and another man entered the lockup area. Mike frowned when the man approached the bars.

"Hello. I'm Mark. I'm the medical examiner. I need to get a sample to prove who you are." Mark held up a cotton swab.

Mike shook his head, "I'd rather call a lawyer. He'd tell me you can't have my DNA."

Mark shook his head, "Fine. I'll get the Chief. He'll straighten this out."

Mike watched Mark as he left the room and went down the hallway. He felt the rage rumbling in his gut. If only Mary hadn't moved way out here, he'd still have his old job. His current employment was nuts.

Heavy footsteps came down the hall, and Mike looked up. Joe was standing with another officer and pointing at him! Mike almost smiled. Good ole Joe, he thought. He came through.

"Yes, Chief. I'm here to escort this man to the Coast Guard offices. They want to interrogate him." Joe said.

The other man nodded as he studied Mike's face. He nodded, "Let's get the paperwork settled first, Joe. I didn't know the Coast Guard hired temporary officers."

Mike's heart sank. Joe wasn't working for the Coast Guard, was he? He better not be. And why did the Chief stare at him like that?

Mike looked up when he heard footsteps again. That Mark guy went past the lockup and back to his own place. He sure hoped that was a good sign.

Mike jerked when he heard the keys jangling in the lock. He couldn't believe he'd fallen asleep. How long had it been? But there was Joe, the Chief, and that other officer, opening the door.

Mike began to stand up, but the other officer shook his head, "Sit back down, Mike. We are just providing you with a roommate."

Joe glared at Mike as he was propelled into the cell. The door closed behind Joe, and Mike stared, "What? What's going on?"

The Chief smiled, "We'll let Joe explain it to you." Then, he and the other officer walked away.

Joe stared at the men leaving and then waited a minute before turning to Mike. "What were you thinking? I told you to stay away from that woman."

Mike frowned, "But why are you in here? What happened?"

Joe rolled his eyes, "I was told to get you out of here. But you just had to ruin it." He scoffed and slammed the wall with his hand.

"How did I ruin it?" Mike asked as he stood up. He bunched his hands into fists and glared at Mike. "I was just sitting here."

"You did something. The Chief knew that you and I were working together. How else would he know that? You told him, that's how." Joe spit out the words.

Mike looked at Joe in shock. "No, I didn't talk. I still can't believe you roped me into this. Those other guys have no idea how danger-ous the gang is. I do. And I'm getting out while I can. I'll just go back to Ventura and forget I ever knew any of you."

Joe snarled, "If only. That's not going to happen. They know how to find you and your precious little Mary. They have no problem eliminating loose ends. Trust me, you don't want to cross them."

Mike's eyes glazed over. He racked his brain for ways to disappear. He'd have to pack up and drive out of California. Maybe he could make it to Toronto. He'd have to change cars, change his name, and...

"It won't work, Mike. I've tried to figure out what to do myself. The only way to leave the gang is to die. And I don't want to die. I hope Wilson doesn't know about the gang. That would be bad news for this town." Joe said.

Mike looked at Joe, "Well, thanks, buddy. You sure did me a favor reading me in."

"How soon do you think they'll move us?" Joe asked.

"What do I care? I'm gonna die anyway, no matter where they put me." Mike complained.

"Maybe we can escape from the Coast Guard?" Joe wondered.

Mike turned his back on Joe and fell into a troubled sleep.

Chapter 22

Mark and the Bodies

Mark stood before Wilson's desk, "This is the report on the two autopsies. The woman has a gash on the back of her head. Her lungs were filled with water from the bay. Do we know who she is yet?"

Wilson looked at Sharon. Sharon shook her head, "The mayor is still recovering. He only got through half the list of competitors. I gathered the list from him and brought it back here. I need to get started on it."

Wilson sighed, "Okay. I guess we'll wait on that. What about the man?"

Mark slumped into a chair. "He's a little more difficult. I think he was bitten."

"By a shark?" Wilson asked.

Mark shook his head, "I think by a whale. They rarely bite anyone, so I've contacted a marine specialist."

"Hmm," Sharon began, "Larry was taking pictures of the competition. He might have gotten a picture of the boat accident."

Wilson nodded, "Give me the list from the mayor, and I'll make the calls. You go check with Larry." Wilson looked at Mark, "Anything else?"

"Was there any report from the Coast Guard on the incident? I'm wondering what they saw." Mark said.

Wilson nodded, "Give them a call, and let's get this figured out."

Mark nodded and disappeared through the door. Sharon stood up, "Mark, wait," She looked at Wilson, "Later, Chief."

Wilson nodded and turned to the list. He picked up his phone and started dialing.

Sharon rushed after Mark, "Mark, wait. What are you going to do?"

Mark turned to Sharon and smiled, "I'm going to call the Coast Guard to see if someone saw anything in the water besides the men and boats. The thing is, the wound isn't really a bite, per se, more of a scrape, a really deep scrape."

Sharon stared at Mark, "You mean like a scrape from the mouth of a whale, baleen, not teeth."

Mark nodded, "Yes, exactly. We had problems with a whale and a boat a couple of months ago. The shark protected the men. Now, a rogue wave attacks a boat trying to escape from the coast guard."

"You think the whale caused the wave?" Sharon asked.

"I think the whale was part of the wave that destroyed the boat. I think it landed in the middle of the boat and crushed it. Then, this man got in the way of the whale's mouth as it swam away. He may have already died from the crushing of the boat." Mark said.

"What do you mean?" Sharon asked.

"He had quite a few broken bones, Sharon. And it looks like he was shot recently. It was beginning to heal." Mark said.

"Shot? These people are dangerous. I should probably call Bart after I check with Larry." Sharon began to leave.

"Just a second," Mark said, pulling her toward him, "I get a kiss, right?"

Sharon laughed, "Of course you do." Then they kissed. "Now I'm leaving."

Chapter 23

Mary and Bart

Sharon said goodbye to Larry and answered her phone, "This is Sharon."

"Hi. Sharon, you date Mark, right? This is Eilene, Bart's wife. I've been released by the doctor, but only if I get a ride home. I've been calling Bart, but he has not answered. I messaged Sarah, but she hasn't responded. I'm getting worried."

Sharon looked around and realized she wasn't far from Mark's building. "I'm not that far from the apartment now. I'll check and call you right back." Sharon said.

"Are you sure? I really hate to trouble you. I'm worried about Bart's old friends. They hang with bad people." Eilene said softly.

"We know about Bart's friends and the gang they hooked up with. We have some of his old friends in jail right now, the ones the Coast Guard doesn't have." Sharon said.

"Oh, okay. Well, let me know, please." Eilene said again.

Sharon said, "Will do," and hung up before she could say more. Sharon shook her head. She turned the corner at the following street and walked quickly toward the apartments. Sharon saw Sarah and a strange dog as she approached the street near the apartments. Her phone rang, and she picked up. "This is Sharon."

Chief Wilson's voice burst out, "Something's wrong. Can you check on Sarah?"

"I can see her right now. She's on the street in front of the apartment complex with a dog. I haven't seen this one before. She looks fine, but I don't see Bart." Sharon said as she jogged across the street. "Sarah, hi, it's me, Sharon, remember?"

"Officer Sharon. Thank you for coming. Some men came and took my Daddy. I've never seen them before. I hid in my dresser drawer. They said bad words." Sarah called as tears slipped down her cheek.

"Chief," Sharon said into the phone, "Bart has been kidnapped, but Sarah hid and is safe. Looks like the gang is planning something."

"Get Sarah into the station," Wilson said.

Sharon said, "Yes, Chief." But Wilson had already hung up. "Sarah, tell me what you heard and saw while we walk to the station. Okay?" Sharon held out her hand, and Sarah gripped it hard.

"Wait, where did the dog go?" Sharon asked.

"I don't know. I've never seen him before. He came into the apartment and found me. Then he helped me pack a bag." Sarah said.

"He helped you pack a bag?" Sharon asked.

Sarah nodded, "He found my backpack and brought it to me. Then he found my tablet, but it was smashed." Sarah hiccuped, "I can't tell my mommy what happened."

Sharon kept walking forward as quickly as she could. "I spoke to your mommy. We will call her from the station. What were you and your Daddy doing today?"

Sarah panted and pulled on Sharon's hand, "I need to find my daddy."

"Chief Wilson is already looking for your Daddy. But I need to know what you know. Tell me your story, Sarah." Sharon said.

Sarah sighed, "Fine. Daddy and I were waiting for Mommy to call. She might get to come home today, but we have to go pick her up. Daddy made some eggs for us while I read my book to him. Then, just as he was putting the eggs on plates, I ran into my room to put away my book. That's when I heard the door break, and Daddy said the hide word."

Sharon's forehead wrinkled, "What's the hide word?" she asked.

Sarah sighed, "I can't eat pineapple, so if Mommy or Daddy say pineapples, I hide."

Sharon looked at Sarah and nodded. "He said pineapples, didn't he?"

Sarah nodded, "Yes. I hid. I quietly squished into the bottom drawer and closed it. I heard feet pounding on the floor, bad sounds, and Daddy moaning. Someone entered my room and looked under the bed and in the closet, but they didn't see me. My Daddy yelled that he didn't know anything and couldn't tell anyone anything. But as his voice got further away, he started singing."

"He sang?" Sharon asked. Sharon guided Sarah through an alley so they didn't have to walk on a busy street. She knew they were almost to the station.

"He started singing nursery rhymes. I don't know why. He sang the last half of Mary Had a Little Lamb. So, she had a little lamb as white as snow. And then he sang, Are you sleeping, are you sleeping, sat on a tuffet, eating her curds and whey." Sarah sang the words to the correct tunes.

"That sounds like he was sending you a message, Sarah. Did he sing anything else?" Sharon asked.

"Just had a great fall, and then he groaned again. Car doors were slamming, and a car drove off." Sarah said.

"Just one car?" Sharon asked as she pulled Sarah toward the back door of the station.

"Yes, just one car," Sarah said. "So the clues are Mary, brother John, the spider scared her, and Humpty Dumpty."

Sharon pulled Sarah into the back door and locked it. She grinned at Sarah, "Great work, Sarah. Thank you."

Julian ran down the hallway and slid to a stop in front of Sharon. "Mary, did you see her? She's not answering her phone, and her local boss hasn't seen her. She's late for her shift."

Sharon nodded, "Bart saw Mary as he was taken. There's a John and a spider involved."

Julian's mouth dropped open, and Sarah said, "Don't forget Humpty Dumpty."

Chapter 24

Donner and Susie

Donner sat with Susie, hunched behind the bushes in the alley. "I don't see why we can't just walk up to the front door and around the house. We're dogs. Who's going to notice us?" Susie huffed.

"We are big dogs. People notice big dogs. Besides, Cecil has some seagulls listening in." Donner said as he stared at the back of the house.

"I wonder why no one noticed when they arrived with Bart and Mary. They weren't quiet." Susie barked softly.

Donner shook his head, "This part of town is mostly rentals. And most of them are empty right now."

Susie shook her head, "I wouldn't want to live this close to the plant. Why don't they take down those big towers?"

"Usually, people look at the rock in the bay and the ocean. I wouldn't want to live here, but tourists aren't that picky." Donner huffed quietly.

A seagull landed between Donner and Susie, "Finally," Susie muttered.

The seagull eyed Susie and shifted closer to Donner. "Okay, they are arguing constantly. Mary and Bart are in the same room. Both are tied up and lying on the floor in one of the bedrooms. The guys are in the kitchen slash living area, popping open beers and eating sandwiches."

"No one is watching Mary and Bart?" Susie asked.

"No," the seagull said, "They are eating, drinking, and arguing."

"What's the argument?" Donner asked.

"What to do with Mary and Bart? Trade them for Joe and the other guy or the ones the Coast Guard has. Mostly, they want the Coast Guard guys. No one agrees on anything. But one guy is huge and sits there eating and drinking." The seagull said.

"He's not arguing. Hmm, so he's the boss?" Susie said, "Are they still arguing?"

"No! The big dude slammed down his bottle and yelled, 'Enough. Where's the stash?" The seagull said.

"Did anyone know where the stash is?" Donner asked.

"One guy said at the bottom of the bay. He didn't think the Coast Guard had it." The seagull flew away as a truck drove down the alley. Donner slunk down under the bush, and Susie made herself small.

The truck moved slowly past Donner, rolled onto the street, and turned. Donner stared at the vehicle. "Something smells fishy," he said.

An owl landed next to Donner. "Donner, the humans need to know where to find the hostages. We can't locate Festus."

Susie sat up and barked, "What? Where's Festus?"

"Shh, Susie, lie down." Donner looked at the owl, "My Precious, she can type. You know where she lives?"

"She's next door to me, at Nancy's house," Susie said as she crouched down.

"Got it," said the owl as he flew off.

"Where is Festus?" Susie asked.

"He was hiding out at my house sleeping, but if he went home, his human had a costume that made him useless to us," Donner said, watching the windows of the house.

Susie's lips quivered, "What costume would that be?"

Donner grinned, "A beachball."

Susie slapped her paws on her muzzle, trying to contain her laughter. "I don't know. He would be a good distraction."

"Settle down. You are awful at stakeouts. I had no idea you couldn't sit still." Donner huffed.

"I'm worried about Jane. I hope she is okay." Susie muttered. "Wait, she has the frequencies of my implant. She can locate me on her phone."

Donner stared at her, then went back to watching the windows. "I hope the person in that pickup was someone on our side. They may know where we are."

A bright blue bird landed on the bush next to the fence. "Hi. Are you Donner and Susie?"

"Who are you?" Susie asked.

"I'm a mountain bluebird. They call me Bluey. I was sent by Cecil. My Precious typed on the tablet. A heron came and took it to Nancy at the coffee shop. After she stopped screaming, she called the police station." The bird twittered. "The owl sent notice that two humans left the station."

"Thank you, Bluey, for that report. Is Nancy okay?" Donner asked.

Bluey shrugged and flew away.

"Should we move closer to the house?" Susie asked.

"Not yet." Donner looked down the alley. "Julian is creeping close. I bet we move then."

"Okay," Susie pulled her back paws under her so she could leap the fence.

Donner sighed, "Wait for my signal."

Chapter 25

Mark's Party

Wilson looked around the rooms with pleasure. "These apartments are really nice. Lots of room for entertaining."

Nancy frowned, "But no yard for the pets. And no way to put a pet door in the building door."

"Killjoy," Wilson muttered as Nancy giggled. She patted his arm.

Mark came in from the kitchen, clapping his hands. "Attention! Welcome to my humble home. Sharon wanted to do this gathering here, so Eilene didn't have far to walk home." Mark bowed toward Eilene, who was sitting on the couch surrounded by Bart and Sarah. Mary sat next to Bart while Julian brought her a drink. "We have much to celebrate today!"

A cheer sounded from the group, and a few barks and meows were thrown in. Sharon cast a worried look toward the balcony where many birds sat listening.

"We want to welcome Eilene home from the hospital and celebrate her full recovery. And all the friends she and her family have made this week." Mark said.

Eilene raised her hand, "Hey, I was unconscious for most of that time. Bart and Sarah did all the hard work."

Bart looked at his lap, but Sarah announced, "My daddy helped put away the bad guys. And I made friends with Donner and Festus."

Bart smiled, "And others, like Sharon, Nancy, and Wilson."

Sarah grinned, "Don't forget My Precious."

"Who could?" meowed Festus, flinching as My Precious slapped his head.

Susie huffed as Jane touched her head. "We had a lot of teamwork," Jane said.

Wilson nodded, "Morro Bay runs on teamwork. Everyone pitches in."

"Noah and Olivia have joined us online. Everyone, wave at our friends watching the station." Mark said. "Thank you for working this shift."

Denny sat in a chair next to Larry. "Yes, keep my seat warm. I'll be there in two hours."

"Sounds great, Denny," Olivia's voice came from the tablet.

Nancy asked Denny, "How is your recovery going, Denny?"

Denny brightened and sat up straighter, "My doctor cleared me to work an entire shift now. He said I just needed to relax and ease into it."

Larry nodded, "That's always important. I have trouble relaxing sometimes. But not when I'm taking photos." Larry pulled up his camera and snapped a few pictures. Everyone laughed.

Mark waved his arms, "Food is ready, so grab some plates and fill them up."

"Were Larry's pictures helpful to the case?" Mary asked as Julian left her side to get her a plate.

Sharon nodded, "Yes, they were invaluable. He caught the boats as the wave hit the entrance. It revealed a whale in the wave."

"Wow, a whale?" Mary asked, "That sounds scary."

"It looked scary," Wilson said. "The whale landed on top of the boat, smashing it. Turns out that's what happened to the male body Julian pulled in. His bones were broken by the whale's weight, and then the whale's mouth caught his body briefly."

"He was bitten by a whale?" Sarah asked. "Wait, what kind of whale was it?"

Mark smiled, "You are right to ask, Sarah. It was a baleen whale, so it had no teeth. The man's skin was pierced by the whale's baleen. The whale did not bite the man. He probably spit him out."

"I wonder why the whale was in the wave? That doesn't sound like something a regular whale would do." Sarah said.

"The Coast Guard said the boat had been used to kill whales further south. When the gang moved north and met with Bart's old friends, they offered the ship to distribute up the coast.

On one of their trips, they stashed a large amount of product on the other side of the Rock." Sharon said. "The Coast Guard has had that boat under surveillance for the last year in connection with the whale killings.

Apparently, the whales had been watching the boat too. When some original gang members boarded the ship, the whale made sure they were stopped."

"But why did they kidnap Mary and Bart? How would that benefit the gang?" Eilene asked.

"That's the interesting thing. Mary's ex was in jail with the latest bad cop, Joe. The gang wanted to get them away from jail to eliminate them. But they also wanted the guys the Coast Guard had. Turns out they were gang members." Sharon said.

"Bart actually gave us a series of clues as he was being kidnapped. He knew Sarah was hiding, but could hear him. So he sang pieces of nursery rhymes, knowing Sarah could remember them all." Sharon continued. "And Sarah did remember them all."

Sarah's little voice sang out, "She had a little lamb that was as white as snow. Are you sleeping? Are you sleeping? Are you sleeping?

Are you sitting on a tuffet, eating her curds and whey? Had a great fall."

Eilene watched Bart's face as he grimaced. She patted his arm. Bart smiled at Sarah. Festus meowed when My Precious snuggled closer to him. My Precious purred loudly.

Julian handed Mary a plate. "Imagine my surprise to hear Mary's name down the hall. I'd been trying to reach her for over thirty minutes. There were Sharon and Sarah in the back hallway talking about clues."

"But what were the clues?" Larry asked.

Denny nodded, "Good question, Larry."

Sharon smiled, "Bart told us he saw Mary, and he gave us the names of the men who kidnapped him: John, Spider, and Hump. We identified the gang with that information and a call to the county sheriff's office. We coordinated with the Coast Guard, who revealed that the two men they had were scared of the gang. They wanted to stay locked up."

"Then Nancy had a visitor in the coffee shop," Wilson grinned.

Nancy put her hands on her hips and glared at him. "It's not every day a giant bird walks into the shop with a tablet in its mouth."

"A giant bird?" Sarah asked, "What kind was it?"

Nancy smiled at Sarah, "I'm told it was a heron. It left the tablet on the counter and waited for me to pick it up. When I pulled out my phone, the bird turned around and left. My voice was still shaking when Wilson answered."

Sarah bounced on the couch, "What did the tablet say?"

Nancy laughed, "It said, My Precious here. Human, call Donner's human and tell him to get his men over to save Mary and Bart. The rest was the address."

Sarah giggled so hard that she slipped off the couch. Then she walked over to My Precious and hugged the astonished cat. "Thank you for saving my daddy for me."

Then Sarah went back to her mother's side. My Precious sat stunned for a few seconds, then she began grooming her fur, muttering, "Now my fur is a mess."

Festus wisely said nothing.

"I went through the alley in a pickup and saw Donner and Susie there behind some bushes. So I reported to Wilson and parked the truck on the side street. I walked back to where the dogs were. But Susie hopped the fence before I could reach them." Julian said.

Sharon took up the tale, "Donner jumped the fence to stay with Susie and left Julian to figure out where to hide from the house. Meanwhile, Wilson and I moved in from the front of the house. When we reached the porch, Susie and Donner barked wildly. We watched the men move to the back door. While Festus and the dogs kept their attention, Sharon and I entered the house and led Bart and Mary out the front door."

"Festus was there? How did he distract the men?" Sarah asked.

Donner and Susie began huffing as if they were laughing. Wilson grinned, "Pete put Felix in a new costume his girlfriend made especially for him. He was a beachball."

"But, how did he get there?" Sarah asked.

Wilson smiled and said, "Seagulls. About ten stuck their talons into the ball and carried Festus to the backyard. He'd been trying to run away from Pete at the time. Just imagine a bunch of seagulls flying a beachball across town."

"Too bad I wasn't there. I could have gotten a picture of it. Now, no one will believe it." Larry said.

"By the time the seagulls dropped Festus into the backyard where Donner and Susie were barking, the ball had deflated enough that Festus could run. Donner and Susie chased him around the yard while the men looked on. They thought it was hilarious." Julian said.

"At least until the state police, county sheriff's officers, and the Coast Guard pulled up at the house. They were surrounded and arrested in a matter of minutes. No shots fired." Wilson said.

"Donner and Susie jumped the fence with Festus, and we ran for my pickup. I gave them a ride back to the station." Julian said.

"The crime scene was held by the state police until the feds showed up." Sharon finished. "And Mary and Bart were taken to the clinic for medical care."

"Sharon called to tell me what was happening, but it was too late. The doctor said I needed to spend another night. He wanted me to have one more night of sleep before I entered the fray back here." Eilene said.

"But you are home now, mommy. And we will all take a nap when we finish eating, right?" Sarah asked.

Everyone laughed and continued to visit. Donner nuzzled Susie as she leaned into him. My Precious touched Felix's nose with her paw. Nancy exchanged smiles with Wilson. Mark brought a plate to Sharon to eat. Julian refilled Mary's cup and then finally got himself a plate. Eilene smiled at Bart as she hugged Sarah. "A nap sounds delightful, Sarah."

Olivia's voice came out of the tablet, "Hey! Denny. Can you come in early? We have a disturbance at the Rock."

Denny jumped up and set down his plate and cup. "I'll be right there."

Sharon called, "Do you need anyone else?"

Noah appeared, "I'll head up there with Olivia. Just some people arguing and shoving at the Rock. We can handle it."

Denny called, "ETA 5 minutes," and ran out the door.

Wilson sighed, "Never a dull moment."

What's Next?

In book 3, The Sacred Rock, discover what happened at the rock. What new adventures will Wilson, Donner, and Festus find?

Check out the Morro Bay Mysteries Cozy Mystery series page for updates.

Thank you for reading

The best thing you can give an author is an honest review of their book. Tell me what you really think and leave a review here or where you purchased this book.

More About Anna

Anna is the mother of three adults, and she has been happily married for over thirty-five years. She invested over six years in schooling her children at home. Then she volunteered at the local high school for ten years. She has a two cute grandsons. Three cats strive for premium napping space near her as she works on her computer.

APCreationsHub.com

For free Daily Prayer Guide, see APCreationsHub.com/daily-prayer

Download Free Books!

Books by Anna

Emily's Cat Mysteries – Cozy Mysteries full of Heart, Fun, and Faith

- Discovery: Finding Home
- The Spider Knows: Helping Neighbors
- Lost and Found: A Community of Hope
- Violet Says Goodbye: Holiday Love
- The Wolf and The Coyote: Going Home
- The Search for Norm: Home Sweet Home
- Recovering From Trauma: Getting Back Home

- Morro Bay Mysteries: Donner and Festus (Prequel for Morro Bay Mysteries)

- Robbie and the Hummingbird: The Romance Begins

- Susie and the Lizard: He Makes Wrongs Right

- Myra and the Kittens: He Provides While They Sleep

- Dorothy Comes Home: Is It Love?

- Get Books 1-8 as a box set (eBook only)

Morro Bay Mysteries – Small Beach Town Cozy Mysteries

- The Rocky Start

- On the Rocks

- The Sacred Rock

Planted Flowers Christian Romantic Suspense series:

- Lily

- Iris

- Violet

- Camellia

- Jasmine

- Rose

- **Planted Flowers Bible Study Workbook**

- **How Planted Flowers Began and Other Stories**

- **The Detective (Bridge to Matthews' Matchmakers)**

Matthews' Matchmakers Christian Romantic Suspense

- **The Vocalist**

Daily Prayer Guide series:

- **Daily Prayer Guides**

- **Daily Prayer Guides Volume 2**

- **Daily Prayer Guides Volume 3**

- **Daily Prayer Guides Volume 4**

- **Daily Prayer Guides Volume 5**

- **Daily Prayer Guides Volume 6**

- **Scriptural Affirmations**

- **The Three Ps Prayer Book**

- **Daily Prayer Guides Volumes 1-6**

Children's Books

Charlie's Picture Books

- I Am a Medieval Cat

- I Am a Christmas Cat

Charlie's Storybooks – five stories

- Charlie Gets A New Home

- Charlie Gets A Girlfriend

- Charlie Moves to Texas

- Charlie Gets A Puppy

- Charlie Gets A Kitten

Charlie's Chapter Books

The Adventures of Charlie and Ginger

- The Case of the Missing Fur

- The Case of the Missing Heart

Driving with Anna Devotional series – Life with Teenagers

- Surviving Life

- Surviving Work

- Parenting

- In Search of Me

- Loving Family

- Friends

- Driving

- Beginnings

Other Devotionals

- Be Strong and Courageous

- Remembrance

- Pray Specifically Journal

Affirmation Journal series:

Three Sizes, Pocketbook 5x8, Desk size 8x10, Offered in Paperback, Kindle, or Editable PDF versions

- **Envisioning Goals**

- **Finishing Goals**

- **Hiding Place Goals**

- **God's Love Goals**

- **Compassion Goals**

- **Grace and Mercy Goals**

- **Hope Goals**

Made in United States
North Haven, CT
19 January 2026